The
Zero Mass Machine

by

J. R. Murphy

First Edition: May 2011
Printed in the United States of America
ISBN 13: 978-1461135715
ISBN 10: 1461135710

To Freeda,
for her editorial work

PROLOGUE

The decades surrounding the late nineteenth and early twentieth centuries held many surprises for the scientific community. Relatively little was known at that time about the nucleus or core of the atoms that make up all things. Einstein showed us the awesome power that could be released simply by manipulating the particles within it.

Knowledge accumulates over the years, so what is thought to be fact now may be proved wrong -- even as early as the next decade.

Conventional wisdom tells us that all matter is constructed of a nucleus and various combinations of electrons in orbits around it, a microcosm, if you will, of our own Solar System.

At this time, the zero mass atom described herein would be as impossible as traveling backwards in time or achieving the speed of light.

Gravity, we are told, is a constant, a natural law, a force that cannot be altered in any way.

But can gravity be defeated?

Only time will tell.

-JRM

Table of Contents

-1-

The large room was bright, illuminated by several rows of long fluorescent lights. In the center, a group of workbenches, tables, chairs, and equipment had been moved to make room for the demonstration.

Two men sat quietly in straight-backed chairs, their expressions sullen, their movements showing the beginnings of impatience. One glanced at his watch, then joined the other to stare at the object standing in the center of the cleared space.

The device from a distance resembled a vacuum cleaner or a garden tool, but the two men were anticipating a function quite apart from those implements.

An aluminum-looking box, dull gray in color and approximately the size of a large box of cereal, lay flat, silent and motionless. Protruding from its top was a metal pipe fitted with a T handle. Next to the pipe stood a small cylinder, resembling a beer can, with a domed top. Wires and hoses snaked across the floor, connecting the device to a small cabinet at the edge of the demonstration area.

As if on some invisible and silent cue, a tall, neatly-dressed man stepped through a doorway and walked to the seated men. He looked much younger than his age, mainly due to his casual dress and his stalwart posture.

"Good evening, gentlemen," he greeted, his voice ringing across the vast space. "Thank you for coming." He donned a pair of glasses as though preparing to read.

The two said nothing as their eyes followed the big man as he walked up to the device.

Stepping upon the metal case and gripping the handles firmly, he glanced over to insure that his audience was watching. Then, manipulating controls as one might start a blender or microwave, the platform upon which he stood hissed softly. Then a soft buzzing sound was heard.

Slowly, gracefully, the apparatus began to rise.

The two spectators leaned forward in their chairs and watched with interest as the platform continued to rise until the big man's head was just brushing the ceiling. There was an additional hissing sound as he turned the object to face the spectators. He then propelled himself forward until he was floating directly above them.

As he smiled smugly, his fingers manipulated the controls and the platform slid silently back to the center of the area before descending slowly and finally coming to rest on the floor.

He stepped off and produced a smile that was friendly but cautious. "Questions?"

"How high will it go, please?" one of them asked. He was the taller of the two, a thin man with a staunch posture and a coal black beard circling a dark face that was punctuated with hard black eyes.

"It will rise until its occupant runs out of oxygen and passes out," came the reply. Then, noticing that his levity was lost on them, he smiled apologetically. "Certainly higher than the highest building in the United States," he added.

"Is it hard to -- fly?" the other asked. His voice was weak but showed the ease of authority.

"Takes a bit of practice, but no harder than, say, riding a bicycle," came the answer.

"And, how long may one stay – aloft, is it?"

The demonstrator cleared his throat and pulled off his glasses. "That's rather hard to say. At the moment, I would estimate that with the fuel I have and based on two-hundred units, each could rise at an altitude of several hundred feet and remain for fifteen minutes."

The two men nodded in a way that indicated satisfaction. "And where does this fuel come from?" one asked, his eyes fixed on the device.

The host flicked his eyes upward then smiled smugly. "Outer space," he said.

Ignoring the answer as either absurd or more American humor, the two men came forward and looked curiously at the cable and hose. "And these?" he pointed, frowning, "do they not drag behind?"

The host laughed nervously. "No. They will not be needed in the final product. This is a prototype – a test unit, so to speak – so the setup is rather, er, primitive." His eyes searched the two men for signs of understanding.

"I see," one finally commented.

"Then, this . . . final product you speak of will be completely free of all these . . . things?"

"That is correct. Notice, too, that the handle mechanism will unscrew down here," he pointed to the base of the upright, "and the cable can be unplugged here." He again pointed downward.

The shorter man's smile was more curious than friendly. "This makes them easy to, how do you say, transport?" His question was more of a statement.

"Very easy. In fact, one might, uh, transport the cases separately, then assemble them when needed." He raised his eyebrows as though inviting comment.

"Two more questions, please."

"Of course."

"What is the price, and when will they be ready?"

With a calculating look at each of them, the host paused before speaking. The room was silent and the suspense obvious.

"The price is one million American dollars each for two hundred units, delivery in ten months from this date."

With a slight bow, the two men politely backed away a few feet for privacy, then spoke to each other in low tones.

The big man began unplugging the tether. He unscrewed the pipe and unplugged it. After placing the device and its handle on a nearby table, he moved the cables back then swiped his hands together.

The two buyers, dark in both skin and disposition, came forward. "We will expect a final demonstration before the money is released. This is acceptable?"

"Of course," the man agreed. "I shall demonstrate the final product by November tenth of this year, and, I am confident you will be pleased. At that time also I will expect proof that payment was deposited for me in a Swiss bank in the amount of two hundred million dollars. Is that agreed?"

"It is agreed," one stated, the other confirming by nodding.

Understanding that the business was concluded, the big man wasted no time and quickly led the two buyers across the room, around the many tables and benches, to a single door in the rear, which he held open as they passed.

Outside, the night was cloudy and dark, lighted only by a dim halo around the Moon. Just beyond the doorway, a parked limousine sat with its motor idling, steam wafting from the exhaust pipe. As the two approached, a young, uniformed man stepped up and rigidly opened a rear door, then closed it when the occupants disappeared inside. A moment later, the big car began a sweeping turn and followed a small driveway around the side of the huge building, then circled a large empty parking lot in front. One of the men inside the car looked curiously but uninterestingly at the long sign spanning the front entrance. It read:

ROSSITER DYNAMICS, INC.

-2-

For one-third of a second, slightly longer than the blink of an eye, the meteor traced a bright arc across the southern sky.

Among the billions of heavenly bodies, from giant suns to tiny sand-size particles, this rock-like traveler is unique, for its name is determined by its location; when it races through the Cosmos, it is called a meteoroid, when burning in the Earth's atmosphere, it is known as a meteor. If it survives the intense heat and lands, it becomes a meteorite.

Another unique quality of this astronomical body is the effect it has on its watchers. From the deeply distraught to the blissfully happy, that brief streak of light blocks out time and stops all thought. It provides a tiny respite from life, from everyday troubles and anxiety. Even those contemplating suicide are put off briefly, love is suspended for that brief instant, and the curious and those who enjoy the mystery of space are sent into lengthy theoretical speculation.

This magical streak of light, this momentary lapse from reality, with the entire Universe as a backdrop, caught the attention of two men, separated only by some seventy miles within the mountainous terrain of central West Virginia. To them the approach was quite different, for they were near the point of impact.

The meteor first appeared to each of them as a tiny white dot that quickly grew in size and intensity to a brilliant ball of fire. It suddenly curved to the east and illuminated the night sky like a huge falling flare speedily disappearing behind a mountaintop. As quickly as it began, the light was gone, and the night sky returned to quiet blackness, illuminated only with tiny points of flickering starlight.

Tyler Bridges had watched the event raptly. His dark eyes continued to stare at the exact point where the intensely white ball had vanished. His expression, usually in a preoccupation state -- for he had the stern visage of the absent-minded professor -- had taken on a look of hopeful interest. His eyes narrowed, straining to record the exact vanishing point on the terrain.

Witnessing the event had been pure luck. He had stepped outside for some fresh air and was standing on his front porch only a moment before. Aware of the coolness of the night, he turned with purpose and went inside. He looked at his watch. It was exactly 9:20.

His front room was small and efficient, furnished with three chairs placed around a rustic style table, two plush recliners, and a flowery sofa that Lori Dennison hated. Shelves, made of planks and blocks and sagging with books, stood along the rear wall. Near the center a hanging light fixture bathed the room with warm light. A large wood burning stove, its dull black pipe penetrating the 20-foot high ceiling, stood in the center. There were two large windows in the ends, and two smaller windows along each side, all overlooking a small yard surrounding the A frame type cabin. Trees on all sides stood like giant fence posts guarding the forest beyond.

As Tyler came in, the phone rang.

"Hello. Oh, Hello, Mister Hawkins."

"Tyler, your notes are way overdue."

"I know, sir, but if you could give me just --"

"I'm sorry, Ty, but the board is insisting on payment. And since you won't finance --"

"With Mom's expenses, I can't afford to --"

"Sorry, Ty, I can't hold them off any longer."

"I understand, Mister Hawkins. How long?"

"Thirty days, I'm afraid. Foreclosure has already been started."

Tyler hung up and sat down hard, looking around at his surroundings as though seeing them for the first time. The excitement of the meteor waned quickly. Unless something was done soon, all this would be taken and he would be homeless – and other people would suffer.

Bridges had helped build his house five years ago, financed with short-term notes, and he had hoped to live a comfortable existence, enjoy his friends, his mother, and pursue his hobby of geology.

His mother, however, had been sent to a cancer treatment center only two months ago when Tyler was unable to give her proper care at home.

Then, as if on some cosmic timetable, his financial world crumbled when he found out recently that the company he had invested in with the money he had planned for his home, had gone bankrupt. Everything he had worked for these past ten years was gone, placing him into deep debt with no funds to help him dig out.

Retrieving a log from the pile of firewood in the corner, he chucked it into the tiny flames of the stove. Soon, the chill of the room began to disappear.

Cold weather came early in Elkins, West Virginia, for the town stood at the edge of the Allegheny mountain range at

3000 feet above sea level. Tyler worked as a chemist for the state, and had built his house a few miles south of the city because of the proximity to his work. He had worked at the fish hatcheries there since graduating in 1988 with a degree in chemistry and a minor in hydrology. His work did not require a degree, therefore did not pay well; but the area was his home, and his mother was old and ill, and needed him.

He scratched his tousled hair while swiveling his head in confusion, looking for his compass. As he spotted the instrument protruding from a stack of magazines in the corner, the phone rang.

He retrieved the compass and studied the precise instrument as though never seeing it before. Finally he became aware of the ringing and slowly, thoughtfully picked up the receiver. The female voice on the phone had a patient tone to it.

"Ty? It's Lori. You want to fly up north with me Saturday morning? I'm taking some supplies to Connellsville. Weather should be nice -- and we can get married there."

Tyler continued to study his compass. Finally he answered. "Uh . . . what?" he mumbled.

He heard a benevolent sigh, then the voice said: "Oh, never mind. I'll be right over and we'll talk about it. OK?"

"Oh, yeah. Sure. C'mon over." He hung up and went outside.

Standing on his porch, Tyler looked up into the heavens and his eyes traced the path of the recent meteor and came to rest at the exact spot where the flaming ball had dropped from sight. He scratched his head. If he could retrieve that meteorite, maybe, just maybe . . .

He sighted his compass carefully and repeated the procedure before finally noting the reading. Then he shivered at the brisk night and went back inside.

Tyler Bridges' mind had always worked slowly and methodically, contemplating at length every move he made. It was as though his every thought went through some mysterious process before prompting any action. He was – if it was possible to be -- ruthlessly tenacious, a quality that up to now had been of great benefit to him. Nearly everything he attempted, from the difficult to the elementary, no matter how complicated or how time-consuming, he would solve it eventually. He never let go until he mastered, won, resolved, rectified or fixed even the most trivial puzzle or project. And when he wasn't figuring out real life problems, he would flop into his easy chair and begin filling in the numbers of a difficult level Sudoku puzzle.

Focusing on the situation at hand, he rummaged through a stack of magazines and catalogs and finally extracted his Gazateer, a book that contained maps of a topographical nature, used mainly for hiking and biking generally, even though its accuracy would be accepted easily by any geologist. Tyler's copy was worn and wrinkled, the results of rough usage while helping to navigate streams and find access roads to fishing holes.

As his finger traced the map slowly, Tyler studied the terrain to the south as seriously and completely as a doctor would study an x-ray.

Reaching absently for the telephone, Tyler glanced up from the map just long enough to punch the numbers. He laid the receiver down and continued to study the map. Only after he heard a voice squawking did he pick up the handset.

"Bear? Hey, did you happen to see . . ."

"I sure as hell did," the voice interrupted.

". . . the meteorite?"

"And I've got the exact, and I mean exact, point where she went down." Barry added.

Tyler's eyes widened with enthusiasm. "That's just great, Barry. I hope you know that I must find it! The bank called again --."

"Well, since you won't take a loan from me, if you give me a half-accurate azimuth from your location, I can triangulate it and help you find it. My first impression is that it came down directly between us!"

Tyler flipped his legs over his plush leather chair and scratched his head. "OK. Let's get together Saturday afternoon and go get it."

"Fine. Great. Now, how about the azimuth, Einstein."

"Oh, yeah." He looked closely at the compass. "It's exactly . . .two-twenty-two point three."

"Man, this thing is close to me. Wait a sec."

Tyler listened patiently, heard some shuffling sounds and footsteps before Barry came back on the line. Tyler smiled, visualizing his friend tromping around his huge mountaintop ranch house in his work boots and his wife Robin fussing and scolding after him like he was a child.

"My calculations show a distance of fifteen air miles from me, and a little over thirty from you! This is great, man? This thing has dropped right into our back yard!"

-3-

Tyler's voice took on a desperate note. "Look, Barry. Seriously, I need to find this rock. The note against my house is long overdue. They gave me thirty days. I might be able to turn this thing into some real money, get me out of debt and save my house, you understand? By the way, don't say anything about this to Lori, OK?"

"I understand, buddy. Mum's the word. We'll find it. Now, don't worry."

The two men made some preliminary plans to meet on Saturday. They went over a checklist of supplies before hanging up.

Tyler had cradled the receiver when Lori Dennison, her cheeks rosy, ushered in a cold blast of air, closed the door quickly and headed for the stove. Lori was a tall girl properly proportioned with a graceful style and a smile that disarmed anyone she approached. She had her blondish hair tied back in her usual ponytail. "You know something?" she asked, kissing Tyler quickly on the lips. "Winters suck a little more each year, don't you think? I mean, I used to like winters, you know?"

"Yeh. Fish are lucky like that."

"Fish? What do fish have to do with anything?" Lori's clear blue eyes twinkled, as they always did when she bantered with Tyler, or when he surprised her.

"Huh? Oh. Fish. I just meant that you can put a fish into water, boil it, freeze it, then thaw it, and the fish will start swimming again. They love cold as well as hot. Wish we could do that."

Lori smirked. "I'm happy for them. Anyway, do you want to fly to Connellsville with me Saturday?"

Tyler scratched his head and returned to his map for a moment then looked up. "Fly where? When?"

Hands on her hips, Lori sighed, then grabbed Tyler at the shoulders. "Watch my lips, you goof. I'm flying to Connellsville Saturday morning, and I want to know if you want to come along. I added forty dollars to the freight charge so you could take me to lunch. How about it?"

"Oh, sure. Yeah." He straightened up and looked down at her then affectionately touched a tiny mole just above her lip on her right cheek. "I'd like that very much."

She raised up on her tiptoes and pulled his head to her, kissing him with passion. Then she looked up at him; her blue eyes glistened as they always did when she was near him.

She looked at the tall, slightly slumped, thin-chested man in front of her, and wondered if they would ever be man and wife. She stared into his dark brown eyes. "Want me to sleep here tonight, Ty? It's, uh, been a while."

"No, better get home. Your father will go nuts if you don't. I don't need that right now."

"Fine," she said, a pout showing on her lower lip. "I'll head back when I warm up." She sat down, feet toward the stove.

Two years ago, Lori Dennison had fallen in love with Tyler Bridges at first sight. They had met when he had contacted her about flying him to various rivers to do water testing. On their first two flights, Lori learned about Tyler's hobby of collecting interesting-looking rocks and his loving support of his Mother. And he found out about her love of flying.

Their first kiss was quite accidental, and came after their third flight, a seaplane flight that began by taking her Piper Cub off from a trailer towed at 50 miles per hour, and landing on the Tygart River just south of the airport. When they returned, the landing was on a stretch of grass that had been watered down for her. She explained to a nervous Tyler that this strange take off and landing process had been used for many years and Lori planned to continue until she could afford a set of wheeled-floats. The plane bumped roughly to a stop and as Tyler helped her out of the cockpit, she momentarily lost her balance and their bodies came together. Tyler drew her close and Lori felt her heartbeat increase as it had never done with any other man. Her knees felt weak and her hands trembled with emotion. She unconsciously wrapped her arms around his neck and they kissed long and hard, her lips warm and moist, her body melting into his. When they stepped apart, she felt weak and a bit flushed, and plodded unsteadily back to the hangar. At that moment, her question about loving him was answered.

On their next three flights, they never talked about the future, their feelings, or anything personal. They simply lived in the moment and enjoyed each other's company. Tyler's jokes, theories and useless information always made her laugh, and his total lack of arrogance and his candid manner was a continual source of pleasure. Even though they had a few dates, mostly movies and an occasional dinner, Lori found herself anxiously waiting for his next charter request. She loved the charters for it was just the two of them along a quiet stream, or being close in the airplane. It was a pleasure watching Tyler work, and the curiosity he exhibited toward everything natural.

Then there was her Dad, who was vehemently against her being with Tyler, arguing that Tyler was nothing but a womanizer, a lone wolf and a loser that would only romance her then dump her like so many pounds of fish at his hatcheries. Despite her efforts to reason with him, the old man would not budge from his position. Lori usually became angry, left the house, and returned only to find her father drunk. The scenario was repeated every few days, and was taking a toll on Lori.

Some months after she had met Tyler, and after shuttling him west to the Ohio River at Moundsville to check pollution, Tyler was delayed, and the two decided that rather than fight the weather and darkness they would stay overnight. They registered at a nearby motel, and as Bridges started to request separate rooms, Lori interrupted and as she spoke to the clerk, her eyes locked on Tyler. "One room, king-size bed will be fine," she stated softly.

Lounging in the cabin, Lori smiled, recalling that night. Tyler had been wonderful, their lovemaking intense yet soft and lengthy. And, she had been completely satisfied. Three times, as she recalled. She giggled softly, and Tyler, his head in a book, glanced up.

On the trip back from Moundsville the next day, and for the first time in her life, Pilot Dennison felt completely and utterly contented. Even now, recalling the memory, she felt her face flush and her heart flutter.

Lori returned to the present and watched Tyler skeptically. "You're obsessing again, Ty. What's going on? What the hell are you working on? Is it your mortgage? Are you worried about something?"

"What? Oh. No. I'm going to try to find the meteorite that landed nearby a little while ago. Barry and I are gonna get together on Saturday. I really want the thing, Lori. It's been a dream of mine ever since college, to examine a meteorite on my own. Besides, it's probably worth some money, if I want to sell it, or maybe write about it," he added quickly. He suddenly looked at her, hoping she would not bring up the subject of his mortgage, which was much more serious than she knew. "Want to come along?"

"A meteorite landed nearby? Cool. Sure. I'm in. If you can wait until I, we, get back, genius. You're going with me to Pennsylvania, remember?"

"Oh, yeah, right. Well, I guess I'll see you Saturday morning. What time did you say?"

"I didn't Einstein, but make it seven o'clock at the airport. Got it?"

"Uh, right. Got it."

The next day was Friday, and Tyler went to work and began his usual tasks at the fish hatcheries along the Tygart River at Bowden. The department of fish and wildlife's main center was located there, but his responsibilities extended far beyond to most of the bodies of water in the state. His territory extended to the Monongahela River to the north, the Elk and Kanawha rivers to the south, and east to the Ohio. His work today however kept him east along the edge of the Mononga-hela National Forest.

Saturday morning, sleepy and ruffled, carrying a cup of coffee, Tyler moseyed into a small hangar at Randolph County airport. As the wide door began rising, he saw Lori pulling the chain in long, sweeping motions. The room was brightly lit and the red and white Cessna was gleaming. On Lori's instructions, Tyler helped push the plane into the morning twilight. Respectfully he watched Lori as she went through her pre-flight.

She wore charcoal gray slacks, black flat shoes and a white blouse with a long-sleeved blue pullover sweater. Her hair was tied back in a ponytail and flopped across her shoulders as she worked.

Professional as she was, and dressed much like a man, there was no mistaking her for one. Even from a great distance, one could easily make out her soft lines and curves. Tyler watched her, admiring the graceful way she walked and respecting her knowledge and thoroughness with her airplane.

He milled around as Lori completed the inspection on all the cables, cowlings, and brackets and only when she had completed her oil and fuel check did she motion to Tyler to climb in.

Tyler bent his frame into the small cockpit and fumbled for his safety belt. In a few moments, the engine coughed to life and they taxied to the active runway.

Once off the ground, Lori made a tight left climbing turn to avoid hitting a mountain, then set course north for Connells-ville. As they gained altitude Lori pointed out the sheen of a light snow above the frost line. "Winter," she said, twisting her face into a comical sneer.

"It's down there somewhere," Tyler announced suddenly, looking back over his shoulder. "I just hope we can find it," he added.

"So what's so important about this rock, anyway? I mean, except its possible monetary value?" Lori asked over the engine noise. "I mean, a meteorite is a meteorite. Right?"

Tyler pulled his eyebrows into a thoughtful frown and he paused, reluctant to speak.

"Come on, Einstein," Lori urged, "what's so special?"

Fighting the urge to tell her of his financial woes, he looked at her a moment before continuing. "I've seen quite a few of these things, but this one, well, it had a special look."

"What special look? How?"

Tyler grimaced. "I didn't see it for very long," he admitted, "but when it veered off right before it landed, I could swear that the debris and gas tail were pointed straight up, not trailing back along its track. The difference was minute, and it was quick, but I saw it."

"So what?"

"That, dear Amelia Earhart, in a logical world, simply can't happen."

-4-

The morning flight north to Connellsville was fast, steady and uneventful. Scattered streaks of thin, stratus clouds stretched above and to the east and soon the soft drone of the Cessna's engine lulled both pilot and passenger into thoughtful silence. Too early for the thermals to develop, the morning air was as smooth as air shocks on a super highway.

Tyler sat back and lazily watched the forests drift off to his right. He glanced at Lori. He was always at ease with Lori. They had flown many hours together over a two-year time span, and for most of that time, he had been aware that she was in love with him.

On their first trip, Tyler immediately sensed that Lori was a great pilot, one of those rare beings completely at home in the air. She had total command of the aircraft; there was never any question about that. Her senses were alive and her touch on the controls was smooth and subtle, her reactions, when necessary, were instantaneous.

On their many jaunts along the rivers and lakes, she would skim the airplane across the water, executing perfect water landings every time, finally allowing the little plane to settle quietly on the water. A quick taxi to the shore, and she would immediately reach in baggage and bring out sandwiches and drinks for a picnic lunch. "Can't let my favorite passenger starve, now, can I?" she would say.

Tyler smiled at the thought.

Lori, at present, was excited, as always, just having Tyler near her. Her eyes sparkled, just as they did when she first met him years ago. When he was around, her smile was perpetual, and her mind was completely and totally content. She sighed and stared out the window as those familiar thoughts of marriage swept by her. Marriage to Ty. Would it ever be? She frowned slightly, remembering their frequent talks about it.

She sucked in her breath and looked at her passenger. "Ty? Can we talk?"

"Sure. What about?"

"Us."

"Oh," he answered, as though knowing what was coming.

Lori checked the instruments, then the sky. "I mean, I don't want to bug you, but I love you, Ty, and I want to share my life with you. I can sell the business, my planes, and we'll have enough to pay for your house and then some."

Tyler smiled. "Look, Lori. You're wonderful and I appreciate the offer. I know it's hard for you to understand, and all this may change someday. The thing is, if I married you, and you did that, your old man would be right, and we would never be happy. Besides, I think that most confirmed bachelors, like me, are men who don't need – don't want -- to share all the intricacies of life with someone. Same as for women bachelors, I'm sure," he added quickly. "As much as I love you and enjoy being with you, I simply don't want the . . .constraints . . . of a marriage right now, and I don't want your money. I enjoy my life, my home, I love my work, and I treasure my freedom and independence. I'll get out of my financial dilemma somehow. OK?"

Lori's eyebrows pulled down and her blue eyes darkened. "In other words, while you truly like me a lot, basically I'm your whore, good for a good screw when you want, but not allowed to share in your life, is that what you're saying?"

"Lori . . .don't go th --"

Lori scoffed. "Maybe I should start charging you! What am I worth?"

Tyler squirmed around in his seat. "Now, Lori, you know that isn't the case. I care very much for you. No, I don't think I love you as you love me, but I would never hurt you. Look, I'm just being honest with you. And, in time, maybe . . ."

"Could it be that you have some irrational fear of a serious relationship? Some kind of mental thing that keeps you from truly loving someone? Dad says you just want pity."

Tyler snorted. "He'd say that. Tell you what. I'll think about that, and you think about wanting to marry to get away from your father. Or maybe you have issues with your father that goes beyond just getting away from him. Maybe you have an unconscious desire to punish him by marrying someone he doesn't like."

Lori sighed and looked outside. "We've had this argument before, Ty, so let's leave it here. I still love you, and my only hope is that you'll learn to love me someday, hopefully soon. Then maybe our fears and our so-called issues will go away."

She scanned the instrument panel before continuing. When she finally spoke, all signs of hostility and anger had disappeared. "And when you finally come to your senses and decide to share your life with me, mister, I'll show you happiness that will make you regret every day of your bachelor life. And," she bent over and kissed his cheek, "you better hope I can hold on long enough, cause you don't know what you're missing. If you think that night in Moundsville was good, then you have some real surprises coming."

Tyler laughed then settled back in his seat, quickly changing the subject. "You sure you didn't put that little beauty mark above your lip with a magic marker?"

Lori laughed. Then she saw his nostalgic facial expression. Hoping that a memory of that night was streaming through his head, she smiled subtly while she peered out the window.

In just over one hour they landed at Connellsville Airport. It was a small airstrip just off Route 219, with one runway and a couple of shell buildings. They unloaded supplies quickly and were back in the sky by 9:40. When they returned they stowed the plane and ate an early lunch at the Elkins airport restaurant, then headed south to meet Barry. Lori wanted to stop by her house to get her supplies, so Tyler waited in the car, mainly to avoid a confrontation with her father.

It was well known that Reid Dennison did not like Tyler, and had made the fact known to him and everyone else within earshot many times. Although Reid flatly denied it – and even became angry when the subject was broached -- Tyler felt strongly that the old man was jealous and possessive and wanted to keep Lori to himself -- and control her as he had when she was a child.

The two had nearly come to blows one night when Lori -- sporting a bruise on her cheek – met Tyler downtown. He was deeply shaken , and Lori used all her girlish charm to prevent him from confronting her father.

"Ty, he gets angry when he drinks, and he misses Mom and he takes his anger out on me. Usually it is just yelling, but tonight he slapped me. I think he regretted it, because he turned like a whipped dog and left the house. That's his apology. Anyway, please let me handle it. OK?"

Although he was visibly upset, Tyler finally agreed, but stopped short of asking her to move in with him. Instead, he made her promise that if she could no longer handle her father, she would tell him.

Sniffing, she agreed, and nothing more was said that night.

Tyler waited. Lori was in the house only moments, which told him that the old man wasn't home, otherwise an argument would have ensued, delaying her, and would have ended with him following her out the door and yelling and shaking his fist until they were out of sight.

Happily, she had changed clothes and was wearing jeans, boots, and a checkered, quilted shirt, and had clamped a jacket and her knapsack under her arm. She climbed in and Tyler headed out, relieved that Reid wasn't home.

The highway south was a narrow, two-lane strip of old asphalt needing repairs, which slowed travel considerably. Speed average at best under ideal conditions was about 25 miles per hour. The road snaked along the eastern edge of the Monongahela National Forest, a 10,000-acre plot protected by the state and used by the nearby state parks. Civilian population along the route grew noticeably sparse with each mile. The road hugged the Tygart River and passed through a few small villages, places identified primarily by a gas station, a post office, and a convenience store.

Lori watched idly as Dailey, then Valley Bend, finally Mill Creek floated by rapidly. Just north of Huttonsville the road wound along the base of a mountain range climbing to the east and flatlands spreading wide to the west. Although midday, the sun cast long shadows along the valley floor, and a cold breeze stirred the leaves.

They crossed Route 92, which led to the Greenbank Observatory. Then, near Elkwater, they pulled off the highway and nosed the car alongside a large, red pickup truck with the words SOUTHERLAND CONSTRUCTION & SURVEYING on the side. The door swung open and a burly, wooly-headed, bearded man in a turned-up collar on a sheepskin coat stepped onto the gravel. In his boots he was taller than Ty, and about thirty pounds of muscle heavier. He slid the cigar to the side of his mouth and grinned widely. He grabbed Tyler's hand in a firm grip and hugged Lori. "When you gonna get this guy to marry you, girl?"

Lori waved the cigar smoke away. "I'm working on it, but, you know, he's such a chicken . . ."

The three of them piled into the truck and talked through the final few miles until turning onto Route 15.

Here, the trees had lost considerable foliage, and loomed somewhat craggy on both sides of the road, and as the miles passed, the hillsides became steeper, the valleys deeper and the road shadier. Tyler studied a map and Lori looked around, fascinated with the deep, purple-shadowed vastness into which they were traveling.

A small branch of the Elk River was to the south far below them, and finally Barry began watching for a place to stop. "We'll pull off here," he finally said, slowing and pointing ahead to a wide gravel spot that was used as a dumping spot for trash. "My calculations show that the object landed somewhere south of here, hopefully not too far."

When they climbed out, Barry recalled how he and Ty had fished near here a few years back. "Steep country. Lori, watch your step," he cautioned. "Nice to see you wore boots. Lots of snakes here, too." He stopped a moment to consider the task ahead before pulling a backpack from the truck bed and shrugging into it. "Got some rope, survival equipment, stuff like that," he announced, and started tromping downward. "Let's go, kids," he urged as he began propelling himself down the steep grade by grabbing tree limbs and hugging the trunks. The couple watched in amazement as his huge bulk traversed the trees, rocks and underbrush with the agility of a deer.

Tyler and Lori started down, helping each other span the trees, trying to maintain their balance. It was slow, tiresome travel, and all three had slipped and fallen a few times before the land began leveling out. Near the bottom Barry spotted the remains of an old railroad trail, used to haul trees to eastern lumberyards a long time ago. In the decades that followed, their descendents were mostly evergreens. The trees were thinning along the level, marshy ground, giving way to ferns and other flora, indicating that a fire had probably swept the area some years back. Small, multi-stemmed shrubs and bushes, tiny, craggly models of their noble ancestors had replaced the giant trees that once stood here.

Lori was exhausted and stopped to rest by bending over and grabbing her knees. She raised her head and listened to the rustling of the leaves and the moaning wind sliding down the slopes. Overhead, clouds were drifting by, placing the valley in intermittent shadow. The smell of wet, marshy grass and leaves permeated the air.

"OK, Lewis and Clark," Lori said breathlessly, "what do we do about the river? And don't tell me to swim."

Barry stretched his back and stood tall, taking in the rich mountain air, his hands on his hips, studying the area ahead. "Let's get a little closer, and we'll take a look. Maybe there's a shallow place where we can cross."

Tyler was looking upward. "That may not be necessary," he said. They looked up as he pointed toward a small limb on a tall Maple tree high on the ridge above. It had recently been snapped off. "I think we just got lucky. I believe our rock came down on this side of the river. Remember the angle was almost straight down."

"Might have been an optical illusion, too," Barry remarked.

Lori was excited, and quickly suggested a standard square search and rescue pattern, one she had flown many times. They adapted it quickly to the area they were in; they would search south to the river, follow the river west 200 yards, then turn north then east, then move inside and repeat the pattern. Both men agreed and they decided on a search swath of about fifteen feet. Tyler and Barry took the outside, Lori in the center. Since they didn't know exactly what they were looking for, they moved slowly. Barry pointed out that the meteorite may have simply plopped in the moist ground and disappeared. In that case, it would be nearly impossible to find, especially in the limited light of the valley.

Lori checked her watch. "Hey, guys, it's almost four. We've only got a couple of hours, at the most. Be dark down here early – or I should say darker."

Within the hour they were moving north from the river when Barry stopped suddenly and pointed toward the inside of their search perimeter. "Look over there!" he exclaimed, and the three broke into a trot toward a barely visible furrow on a narrow slope. The long tract of dirt could barely be seen above the undergrowth and the three followed it down a steep slope to a small valley-like depression. At the bottom was a circular mound of dirt, mud, twigs and rocks.

Against the wall, nearly buried in the debris, lay the meteorite. It had landed on a slope, and had gathered and plowed grass, undergrowth, and mud until it was finally bogged down, sapped of its forward energy.

The three hunters had climbed down to the crest and had stopped, frozen, as though mesmerized by the rock. Finally Lori broke the silence. "It's beautiful," she whispered to no one in particular.

All in their own thoughts, they knelt, scraped some debris away, and examined the stone closely. It was smaller than, but had the general shape of a football. There were small, flat, glass-like facets, shining like mirrors, scattered all around the surface – or what they could see of it.

As though shaken from hypnosis, Barry began shrugging out of his knapsack. "What do you suppose it weighs?" he asked.

"My guess it's maybe only ten or fifteen pounds," Tyler answered, moving more dirt and debris from around it. "Let's see if we can roll it onto our canvas. Be careful, now," he warned. "This thing might be so fragile it will crumble of its own weight. It may be just hollow ash."

The three worked slowly and discovered that the rock was indeed solid and heavy, but not so much that someone couldn't carry it easily. They carefully wrapped the still-warm object in layers of canvas, then transferred it to a sling with handles on each end, something Barry had cobbled together to use for carrying firewood.

By 5:45, the three took a last look around before Tyler and Barry grabbed the handles and started climbing up the steep mountainside toward the truck. They had progressed no more than fifty feet up when Lori, behind, lost her footing and tumbled down, ending up cradled against a tree trunk. She grunted painfully.

"You OK?" Tyler asked, stopping.

Lori laughed and swiped at her pants. "I guess so. Dropped everything out of my pockets, though. Go ahead. I'll pick up and catch up with you."

At the top, the two men had carefully placed the wrapped object in the truck, and were lashing it securely when Lori came skipping across the highway, somewhat muddy and disheveled. After a couple of jokes about being inept and clumsy and her face being dirty, the three headed back toward Elkins.

-5-

On the trip back, Barry dropped Tyler and Lori at the car where they transferred the meteorite and secured it in Tyler's trunk.

Barry stroked his beard in faked concentration. "Now look, guys. Be careful of that thing. We don't know what it is, or what it will do." He raised his wooly eyebrows and looked directly at Lori. "The thing might get you tonight. Maybe you better stay with Tyler for protection."

Seeing her serious look, Barry laughed, shook his head, and waved to his partners while climbing in the truck. Lori thumbed her nose good-naturedly at the big man as he swung around to the highway.

When the two started back, Lori sat in silence a few minutes. When she spoke, her voice had a worrisome note to it. "Dad's getting worse," she said. "I think he's drinking more and gambling more. It's getting harder and harder to live with him." Noticing Tyler's tight grip on the steering wheel, she realized his concern about both her and her father, the latter being more in the area of keeping him from injuring her.

"Anything I can do?" he asked, then, "besides marrying you, that is."

Lori looked at him with a stiff face. "Don't be an ass. It doesn't become you."

"Sorry. Look, I know you love your father. I mean, he's your father. But I'm wondering how he feels about you, Lori. Does he want to keep you near because he loves you, or is it because he wants to possess you, like some kind of pet? Or maybe he just loves controlling you, or trying to, like a puppet."

Lori was staring outside. Finally she looked around. "Well, the thought had crossed my mind." She sighed. "I'll just try to stay away from him for now, I guess."

The two were silent until Tyler turned in to the lane leading to his house. "Ty?"

Tyler looked at her, knowing what was coming.

"I want to stay with you tonight."

He climbed out of the car. "Maybe you better not." Anticipating her question, he continued. "You just said he was getting worse, so why aggravate the situation. No. I'll take you back to your car and you go home. We'll discuss this later, OK?"

"You're about as much help as . . .a . . . fly." She slammed the door and went around to the trunk and began helping Tyler unlash the canvas package containing the rock.

They toted their find across the Moonlit lawn. A chill wind rattled the remaining leaves, and Lori shivered.

They moved around the side and to the rear of the house, coming to an old building with double doors. Tyler indicated putting it down until he opened the large doors. Lori watched in fascination. "Ty? I've never been back here. What a great building. Was it here when you moved here?"

Suddenly the doorway brightened from inside, throwing a lighted rectangle in front. Tyler stepped out. "It was here when I bought the property," he answered. "I first thought about tearing it down, but I needed a place to put my junk, you know, tools and stuff. So I fixed it up, added electricity, and put a new roof on."

Lori looked fascinated and proceeded to walk around, hands behind her. "What a great space," she said as she meandered through the partitions, junk, and machinery. Tyler, smiling, led her out and locked up.

Back at the airport he watched as she drove off after giving him a sisterly goodnight kiss, followed by a long hug. Tyler watched until her car was out of sight.

At his house, Tyler succumbed to his curiosity and returned to the shed. He knelt and looked closely at the facets on the meteorite. Instead of windows, as they first thought, the glassy areas seemed the result of chips broken away, exposing some inner material. He felt sure this was the case since they were flat and not contoured like the stone. Tyler's interest in rocks had led him to study the molecular structure of glass, coal and diamond, all of them members of the quartz family. These kinds of substances would sheer off smooth-faced when broken. Indians made arrows and tools by chipping flint rock along their fault lines. Break a lump of coal and the surface is so shiny you can almost see yourself. He scratched his head and made a quick assessment that the thing was probably just a piece of quartz that had been charred by heat on the outside. He wondered just how much money this thing would bring at an auction. He was sure that somebody would pay a pretty penny for a beautiful amber rock from outer space. Might be worth thousands, even, Tyler assessed. Maybe this was truly the answer to his financial problems.

Yawning, he checked his watch. It was near 10 o'clock, so he locked up both shed and house. After showering then reading for an hour about quartz structures, he extinguished his reading lamp then squirmed beneath the covers.

Sunday morning was bright and cheerful. The Dennison house was quiet. In the large kitchen, Reid Dennison sat, his red-ringed eyes staring blankly, and sipped absently at his coffee. He swung his eyes to his daughter as she entered the room. "I see you were home when I got in last night. Figured you'd be shacking up with Bridges."

Lori poured her coffee, and looked directly at her father, and jutted her chin. "I wanted to, but Tyler wouldn't let me."

"Good God, I've raised a whore," the old man stated sadly.

His daughter placed her cup carefully on the counter. "Look, Dad. I'm not talking loud, because I know you have a hangover. You seem to be hung over most of the time nowadays." She sat down opposite him and looked at his ruffled hair, the flushed face, the bloodshot eyes, and his scraggly beard. "I'm sorry about Mom dying, but Dad, that was years ago. And . . . look at me. I'm thirty years old, I have a nice charter business, I own a couple of airplanes, I'm happy, involved with a good man, and yes, sometimes I share my love with him. And, I'm a good person!"

"So why don't he marry you?"

Lori sighed, showing her weariness of the many times they had had this conversation. "He's not ready yet. When he is, we'll get married – I'm tired of these arguments, Dad. In case you haven't noticed, I pay the bills, I keep the house in good shape, I clean up your messes, and it's my money that keeps us in food."

Her father, surprisingly unruffled by her remarks, got up and refilled his cup. "So where were you yesterday afternoon and evening. They told me that you got back from your charter about noon or so."

Lori shrugged. "If it's any of your business, Tyler and I went down around Monterville to look for a meteorite."

Reid laughed. "You went all the way to Point Mountain to look for a rock? Sounds to me like Bridges is running out of ideas to get you alone in the woods."

"He doesn't need to make up stories to get me alone – anyway, Barry Southerland met us just this side of Valley Head and went with us."

"You find anything?"

"Matter of fact, we did. It's beautiful and Tyler said it might be worth a lot of money."

Their conversation had turned civil, and all disparaging remarks about Tyler's relationship disappeared. Lori told her father about the meteorite and how they had wrapped it and that Tyler had put it in his shed. Her father listened politely and the coffee had sobered him enough that he refrained from further comment.

"I'm leaving now," Lori told him as she gathered the cups. "I have some paperwork at the airport, then Tyler and I are going to take in a movie. I should be home to fix you supper. Will you be here?"

Reid Dennison looked thoughtfully at his daughter. "Probably. Hell, nothing else to do."

Lori left the house in high spirits and had her paperwork finished by noon. To hold her appetite over, she grabbed a quick snack and took a couple sips of coffee at the airport, then headed for Tyler's.

When she pulled into the driveway she noticed the building door open and went in. Tyler was kneeling down beside the rock, examining it with a magnifying glass. "Hi, Lori. Come look at this."

Tyler expounded his theory that the rock was basically a quartz structure that had been melted to a charcoal state on the outside, and that small pieces had been broken or chipped off, maybe when it landed.

Lori listened in fascination. Finally Tyler got up. "C'mon in the house. I'll wash up and we'll head out."

They ate lunch at a steakhouse buffet, then spent some time shopping before heading to a movie, after which they went back to Tyler's.

"You want to come in?" Tyler asked.

Lori snuggled against him and nuzzled his ear. "I'd love to, but I promised Dad I would make him dinner."

Through her nuzzling and kissing, she told Tyler about their conversation that morning, and that maybe some things were solved, at least for the present. She thought, maybe, just maybe, her dad was beginning to accept her relationship with Tyler, at least to the point they could talk about it without her dad getting so angry.

Tyler was skeptical but seemed pleased, hearing the hope in her voice, though disappointed that she wasn't staying. "Well," he said, following a long kiss, "I'm glad you and your father aren't fighting, tonight, at least. You go now, have a

nice dinner, and I'll just stay here and eat bread and water."
He feigned sadness.

"If I had my way, you know what we'd be doing right
now, don't you?"

"Go," he chided lightly.

As her car disappeared, Tyler took a deep breath. When
he went inside the house, for the first time, he had a strange
feeling, one that he couldn't quite put his finger on, an aware-
ness of a certain solitude and aloneness, a disturbing quiet-
ness. He shook the feeling off when his mind returned to
quartz rock structures and the meteorite.

Rummaging around, he found his old college textbooks
on chemistry and physics, and stacked them next to his chair
in preparation for his plan — for the second time — to absorb
their information on molecular structures, particularly quartz.
He was expressly interested on what effect extreme heat
would have on them. Would it make the meteorite so fragile it
would disintegrate at the slightest bump?

After a quick meal, consisting of a peanut butter sandwich, a pickle wedge, and a half can of peach slices, Tyler
scrunched down in a large, plush chair, flipped his legs over
the arm, and grabbed the top book off the pile.

As he opened it, he suddenly wished Gerald Franks was
here to help him analyze this thing. His onetime roommate in
his junior and senior years was a brilliant student, and had
graduated magna cum laude with a degree in physics. Tyler
called him Jer, short for Jerry. He was a medium-height guy
with a narrow, peaked face, a slim nose that revealed his Ger-
man heritage, and close-set eyes that seemed to showcase his
intelligence, and, though quite liberal, his narrow upper lip

marked him as conservative. He had a bizarre sense of humor, a wide disarming smile, and turned out a few times to be a true friend.

Tyler grinned, both in admiration and regret as he recalled the arguments, the confrontations, and the friendship he used to have with this man. He remembered the political arguments in particular, which usually was prompted by Jerry's remarks about the United States government being as corrupt and evil as the Mafia and Hitler put together. These, Tyler remembered, were quite distressful at the time, but the disagreeable moments had been filtered out through the passage of time.

As pleasant, disturbing and intriguing as these thoughts were, Tyler shook them from his mind and delved into the first textbook to begin reviewing topics that had formerly been so familiar. Scratching his head and plucking at his eyebrow, he immediately became absorbed into atomic structure, atomic weights, periodic tables, moles, nuclei, guarks, and the many other topics that he had struggled with, crammed for, and memorized facts about in order to master the subject ten years earlier.

-6-

The village of Green Bank, West Virginia lies quietly near the National Radio Astronomy/ Observatory. The town's schools, a few businesses, a library, a post office and a small residential area are only a couple of miles from the huge complex whose giant telescopes are scattered throughout hundreds of acres of flatlands buried deep within the Monongahela National Forest. One not knowing the territory would easily mistake the land as being in Kansas, Illinois, or Missouri. To the casual observer, the place would resemble a giant football field, with the goal posts separated not by a hundred but by thousands of yards.

Gerald Franks lived in a small, light-blue, ranch-style modular house at the edge of the town. There was room enough on one side for his car, and a small front yard large enough only to be a mowing nuisance for him. His house was sandwiched between two empty lots, once intended for development, then abandoned, now overgrown.

Franks' Sunday shift at the observatory was short. He went in at noon and caught up on some paperwork then had stopped on the way home for a hamburger. Arriving there, he had just opened the bag when the phone rang.

"Yes?"

"Franks? This is Rossiter."

Franks' eyes narrowed. "What do you want?"

"I want the meteorite," the voice said.

"Look, I told you I want no part of you or --"

"Shut up, Gerald. You know what I can do. Want to spend some time in prison?"

"Where's the meteorite?" Franks asked in a bored voice.

"It came down a couple days ago near you. Get the coordinates, and find that meteorite! Understand!"

Franks sighed in defeat. "I'll try," he said.

"Try, my ass," Rossiter said, "you'll find it or else! Call me when you have it."

The phone went dead and Franks slowly hung up.

Gerald stood motionless, dismay and disgust showing in his eyes. Chastisement showed clearly in his eyes. He had hoped he had seen the end of Kyle Rossiter, not realizing that blackmail never ends. Rossiter had found out about an embezling scheme Franks had been involved in many years ago, and had threatened him with exposure.

Had he known there was a meteor strike, Gerald would have anticipated the telephone call. Maybe he could have taken a few days off, disappeared or something. Instead, he was caught off guard. Knowing Rossiter's temper and the lengths to which he would go, Franks felt shivers travel down his spine, imagining what could have happened.

Relieved only by the thoughts that recovering the meteorite was simply a matter of some hard work and inconvenient time spent, he went to the kitchen.

Slowly eating his sandwich, he went over in his head the plans to recover the rock; the materials he would need both to find it then retrieve it. His first step would be to borrow one of the precision GPS units from work. No one would think anything about it, as many of the employees at the observatory had borrowed them for weekend jaunts, hunting and fishing trips, and some even for vacations.

Franks settled in to watch some TV before showering then retiring, and, by the time he was in bed, tomorrow's retrieval of the rock was completely planned out in his mind. He had trouble going to sleep, but finally drifted off when the digits of the clock turned to 11:30.

Gerald left the house at 4:30 Monday morning, and turned into the observatory entrance, drove past the residence halls and pulled alongside the building where he worked. It was a low-roofed structure, and housed much of the equipment used for repairs and upgrades. The room contained cabinets along the walls, and various tables and benches in the center. The offices were through a doorway and hallway at the rear.

Nearly everyone knew where the GPS units were kept, and Franks went directly to a metal cabinet and picked out a unit, and after checking battery condition, pocketed the device and called his friend over at one of the dishes to get the coordinates. He went outside and, suddenly remembering, returned to his office and left a note to his supervisor that he was not feeling well and would not be in today.

Highways within the National Forest were few. Gerald decided to take Route 92 north, even though it was farther from his destination. After a few miles he turned west and headed for Durban just ahead. He ended up far north of his intended destination, but there were no roads leading due west. When he finally reached Huttonsville, he turned south on Route 219.

By the time he reached the Huttonsville prison, the sun was full above the mountaintops, throwing beams of light fluttering through the trees.

Within minutes he reached the Route 15 turnoff. Once on the small highway, he drove unappreciatively and unaware of the tall trees and forests and the steep mountainous terrain until he finally pulled over and stopped. His GPS showed the same longitude as the meteorite's location. From here he knew to stay near to that longitude and move south toward the final latitude. He climbed out, and for the first time noticed the brisk wind, and turned up his collar.

Twenty-five minutes later he was standing at the deep end of the furrow, looking disgustedly at the pile of pushed-up dirt, twigs, leaves, grass and mud – and footprints. Angrily, he stomped around, studying the imprints, finally deciding that there had been three people here. There were three definite sizes of shoes and he came to the conclusion that either one of the men was very small and light, or there had been a woman with them.

Sickened, he climbed out of the depression and stopped. As reality set in, he was suddenly gripped with fear. No meteorite! How could he explain it to Rossiter? He couldn't. Thoughts went streaming through his mind; it wasn't his fault that someone got here first. No. He wouldn't, couldn't be blamed for that. Probably some local hunter or fisherman had just happened to be close by, and picked up the thing as a souvenir. Damn the luck!

Gerald dabbed the sweat on his forehead with his arm. No, these were excuses, and Rossiter would know it but wouldn't accept it. He, Franks, should have known about the meteor shower, for God's sake! He was put at the observatory for just this purpose!

Kyle Rossiter didn't like failures, and the retainer Gerald had been receiving these past years would be in jeopardy, and would surely be terminated. Christ! Rossiter might demand a refund, which would mean he would have to come up with thousands of dollars!

Dejected, he looked around one final time, then started back. When reached the base of the mountain, he looked upward, reluctant to begin the ascent.

He had climbed a few feet when something caught his eye. He moved over to it and reached down and picked up a business card. He read it and smiled. A wave of relief fell over him, a possible reprieve of sorts. Maybe he could retrieve the meteorite after all! The card read:

DENNISON CHARTER SERVICE
Lori Dennison, Chief Pilot
Randolph County Airport,
Elkins, WV

Smiling at the two phone numbers on the back, he crammed the card in his pocket and hurried up the mountainside assisted by a fresh rush of excitement surging through his body.

He drove into Elkins and stopped at the first telephone booth he came to. He did not own a cellphone since radio transmissions in and around Greenbank were not allowed, at least in the areas where he worked.

He considered the airport number, then changed his mind. He would call the home number.

Two rings later a gruff voice answered.

"Yes. I'm trying to reach Lori Dennison. Is she there?"

"She's probably at the airport. Call there."

"Yes, but she wasn't there. I thought maybe she would be home."

"Try the airport later," the voice suggested abruptly.

Gerald decided to take a chance. "Are you a friend or relative of Lori's?"

"I'm her father. Who's this?"

"My name is Gerald Franks, Mister Dennison, and my company's interested in meteorites, things like that. I have reason to believe that your daughter might know something about the one that landed near here last Thursday."

"This thing valuable?" the old man asked.

"Very, Mister Dennison."

"How much?"

Gerald paused, figuring how much he would need to pay for the object. Rossiter would never have to know. Even if he found out, it was Franks' money. In terms of his keeping his retainer all these years, the rock was very, very valuable to him. He tried to remember how much he had in his savings account. He crossed his fingers. "Two thousand dollars."

The phone went quiet and Gerald held his breath. Finally the old man answered: "Cash?"

"Cash." Franks hoped the old man didn't perceive the anxiety in his voice.

"Make it three."

Franks felt his temperature rise, as though the world was closing in on him. But he had no choice. "Three, it is. When can I get it."

Dennison's voice was tentative. "Well, I don't have it right now, but I know where it is and I can have it tomorrow."

"I'll have the cash for you by ten-thirty in the morning. Where can we meet?"

They made plans to meet at the Dennison house at mid-morning on Tuesday, and the two men hung up. Gerald Franks smiled broadly; a huge burden had been lifted from him. He stepped from the telephone booth and whistled until he climbed in his car. It was a beautiful day, the sun was shining, the air crisp and cold, and all was well. As he drove off, he decided to have a nice late breakfast to celebrate before returning to Green Bank.

In the late afternoon he returned home. As he turned in to his driveway, he noticed a car stopping in front of his house. Panic began to set in as he watched the man climbing out. "Hello, Leif," he said in a creaky voice.

Leif Canfield was tall and slim, with a round face and reddish hair swept back. His glasses needed pushed up on his nose. His smile was artificial. "Franks," he stated flatly. "Kyle sent me down to check on progress." His eyes flicked around Gerald's face. "You get the rock?"

"I don't have it right now, but I'll have it by noon tomorrow."

Leif Canfield looked at him disparagingly. "Who has it?"

"Some guy in Elkins has it and will hand it over to me in the morning."

"Maybe I'd better go talk to him --"

"Please, Leif. He's a little skeptical about letting it go. He thinks he can sell it for a lot of money. He's accepted my offer of three thousand – which I will pay myself, since it was my fault. OK?"

After a look of consideration, the tall man nodded. "I'll be here tomorrow same time. Be careful, Franks, and be sure you don't get your body above the rock. We'd hate to lose you." His smile was malicious.

Franks frowned. "You think I don't know that? You afraid I will die before I get the rock to you?"

"Never mind," Canfield answered, "Just be careful with it."

-7-

Reid Dennison looked around the lounge, spotted his friend at the bar, and began making his way toward him. The place was busy for a Monday night, and Dennison nodded to a few familiar faces and sidestepped around a couple who were trying to dance with no music.

"What's happening, Coke," Dennison greeted as he slid on the adjacent stool.

Coker Brookstone was a small, chunky man with a thick neck and sloping shoulders. He looked younger than his 22 years, mostly due to a thick crop of curly brown hair and a pimpled face. He had quick moving eyes, a condition that belied his calm demeanor. His reddish beard, recently trimmed, almost covered a long scar from his ear to his jawbone, the result of a barracks disagreement when in the army. His callused hands gripped his glass mug with care. He returned his friend's greeting and lifted his beer in salutation.

"Let's go outside where we can talk, Coke," Dennison suggested.

They left the bar and the older man led Brookstone to a vacant spot where he stopped and looked around cautiously.

"What's up?" Brookstone asked as his eyes darted around the parking lot.

"In a couple of hours, you and me are gonna steal a rock," Dennison said with finality.

Brookstone scrunched his face skeptically until Dennison explained that it was a valuable rock, and would be easy money and no one would get hurt. He told him of his buyer, and promised Coker a quick five hundred dollars by noon the next day.

"So what do you need me for? Sounds like a one-man job to me," Coker concluded.

"You can keep a lookout. Besides, I'm not sure how much the rock weighs, and it might take the two of us. Three people brought it out, so we should be able to handle it easy." Dennison smiled. "A quick five-hundred for you, Coke. How about it."

The young man shrugged. "I'm in."

Dennison instructed his friend to return to the bar, keep a low profile, sip only one beer so he would be sober, and meet him back at the parking lot at 1:30. Coker nodded understanding and the two men parted company.

Early Tuesday morning it was cold, moonless, and starry. Coker left the bar and walked to the far end of the parking lot to wait as ordered, making sure he was not seen. Moments later, Dennison's car appeared, crept along and stopped only long enough for his partner to jump in. Both men looked around, saw nobody, and sped off.

The bar where Coker was picked up was slightly north of Elkins. Dennison swung south on a four-lane and headed for Beverly, explaining that he wanted to make sure Lori was home. As they drove by, his house was completely dark and Lori's car was in the driveway.

They returned to Elkins and turned east on Route 33. Coker was curious and asked about the meteorite. Reid repeated what Lori had described to him. Much to Reid's annoyance, Coker began explaining how he intended to spend his share.

As they neared Tyler's house, they parked alongside a convenience store and Dennison got out. Coker, according to plan, would wait a few minutes then follow.

When sober, Reid Dennison was a careful man, and on occasions when the theft of money was involved, flawless in both his planning and his execution.

The two joined up at the entrance to a small driveway that came alongside the house. Their footsteps crunched lightly on the shale as they got nearer. Lori had told him the meteorite was in the shed in back on the opposite side, so he silently motioned Coker to follow him. They slipped noiselessly along the tree line and circled around the far side of the shed. It was getting cold and Coker stood shivering, watching the house for any movement as Dennison worked at the lock. After a moment, the tall man slowly pulled one of the giant doors ajar and the two men slipped inside. Dennison snapped on a tiny flashlight and swung the beam around. Only then did they take a step, fearing they would knock something over.

The meteorite's facets shined brightly when the light fell upon them. Coker's face was a combination of curiosity, surprise, and anticipation as he approached the rock. Alongside, Dennison began shucking his jacket. "We'll wrap it in this," he whispered.

Once wrapped, Coker grabbed the slinged object and moved slowly to the door. Outside, they hurried along behind the house and made their way to the driveway. At that instant, Coker froze, yanking Dennison to a stop.

"Reid!" He pointed. "A light. He's awake!"

"Let's go. Hurry! Don't drop it!"

Inside, Tyler had awakened and looked out his loft window just in time to see two huddling forms running along his driveway. He snapped on the lights and hurried to a closet where he kept his shotgun. He grabbed it and ran down the steps and pulled open the back door. The two figures were walking rapidly and Bridges shouted at them. They began to run. He pointed the shotgun in the air and pulled the trigger.

In the quiet of the night, the blast sounded like dynamite, and echoed through the forest. Tyler started to run when he noticed one of the men had fallen. The other, a tall man, grabbed something and began to run.

Tyler approached the man on the ground cautiously. He was lying face down, and did not appear to be breathing. Tyler felt for a pulse, then returned to the house and called 911.

The emergency vehicle pulled into the driveway within minutes and two people jumped out. Tyler stood at the prostrate figure and watched as they turned the body over. Tyler immediately recognized the man. "His name's Coker Brookstone," he informed them. "That's all I can tell you about him. Don't know where he lives."

As they closed the ambulance, the driver started to climb in when Tyler stopped him. "What was it? Do you know what killed him?"

"Don't know exactly," the young medic stated. "Looks like a heart attack."

Tyler started back to the house, then suddenly changed course and started running toward the shed. Seconds later he saw the broken hasp on the door. He jerked the doors open, snapped on the light, and the look on his face showed that his suspicions were confirmed.

The meteorite was gone.

Suddenly all his financial woes and debts returned. Without the meteorite, there would be no money and the bank would foreclose, the credit card companies would cut him off, and his credit rating would be permanently scarred, not to mention that his Mother's care would suffer.

Dejected, Tyler half-stumbled slowly back to the house, his mind clearly fraught with trouble. When he reached the house he had shed the financial thoughts momentarily, and the sudden understanding look on his face would reveal to anyone that he knew who had stolen his meteorite. Reid Dennison! Coker was known to drink and run with him, and Coker wasn't too bright, and could be talked into anything, given the right motivation, such as liquor or money.

Knowing that Lori's father was the thief troubled Tyler, for it could only lead to more arguments, and could strain their relationship to the breaking point. Tired, sleepy, and dispirited, he realized that confronting the old man was not something he wanted to deal with right now.

He curled up in his easy chair with intentions of reading to divert his mind, but within minutes he was fast asleep, his legs dangling over the plush arm. He was restless, and finally stumbled up the stairs and went to bed.

Tyler woke up mad, and broke the news about the theft and Coker's death to Lori in an abrupt fashion that morning. "Lori, who did you tell about the rock?"

"Nobody – well, only Dad. But he wouldn't --"

"He not only would, but he did," Tyler stated flatly. He's the only one who knew outside of the three of us, Lori. It had to be him. Is he at home?"

Lori looked down at Tyler's clenched fists. Her eyes darkened and her voice became remote and cautious. "Look, Ty, I know you don't like him and you never get along, but that's no reason to accuse --"

"I am accusing him. Face it, Lori, he's nothing but a drunk who lives off his daughter. He's been suspected of thefts and has been under suspicion before. He talked Coker into helping him, and now Coker's dead!"

Lori stepped back as though slapped. "I can't believe you're accusing my father of something that you're not sure of. Did you see him do it? Or are you just hell-bent on seeing him punished?"

"No, I didn't, but I know it was him." Tyler put his hands on his hips, and spoke with finality. "You told him where it was, he and Coker stole it – he ran with Coker, you know – and that's my proof. I'll ask you again, do you know if he's home?"

"Ty, don't do this. If you think he did it, tell the police and let them investigate. I can't believe you're being so unreasonable!"

"I'm through steering around him, avoiding him, and being nicey-nice. I'm tired of his insults and calling you a whore." Tyler turned and started out.

"Ty," Lori said, her voice trembling, "if you hurt him, I'll never forgive you!"

Tyler wasted no time driving to Beverly, and was not surprised as he walked up to the house that Reid Dennison was aware of his arrival. Lori had no doubt called him.

Tyler stepped up on the porch. "Where's my meteorite, Reid?"

"I have no idea. You go to Hell, Bridges."

"I know you stole it, Dennison, and you got Coker killed in the process! Now I want that rock and I want it now!"

Dennison took a step backward. "I don't have it. So you can just get the hell out of --"

Tyler hit him. The blow was a vicious right hook that slammed Dennison's cheek, glanced into his nose, and snapped the old man's head sideways. He stumbled backward and fell through the open doorway. Tyler stood at his feet, hands balled into fists. "Where is it!" he screamed.

Blood was running from Dennison's nose. "I sold it!"

"To who?" yelled Bridges.

"I don't . . . someone named . . . Franks!"

"Tyler reached down and grabbed the old man by the collar. "Frank who?"

"No," Dennison choked, "Franks! I don't remember --"

Tyler's eyes narrowed. "Gerald? Was his first name Gerald?"

"Yes . . . I think so."

Just then Lori rushed up. "Tyler!" she screamed, stepping around him. She knelt by her father and looked back. "Get out of here, Tyler, or I'll call the police!"

Tyler saw the tears streaming down her face and mumbled something about being sorry. He backed down the stairs and slowly walked to his car.

As he drove home and as his anger subsided, his thoughts left Reid and Lori and turned to Coker's death. Although the medic had mentioned a heart attack, Tyler found this hard to believe from a man of Coker's age, and the physical condition he was in. He would have believed a death due to liver damage, or maybe a knife wound from a drunken brawl, even a bullet from a jealous husband. But a heart attack? Tyler grunted, thinking of that

At home, he put in a call to Health and Human Services and after a few rings a lady's voice came on the line with all the urgency of a cow in the shade on a hot summer day. Tyler asked her for the coroner's name. She perked up. "The Chief Medical Officer in Charleston appointed Doctor Nettleton only last week, sir. Would you like her number?"

Tyler scribbled the number, thanked her, and hung up. He called the doctor and explained to the receptionist that he was calling about the death of Coker Brookstone.

"Brookstone, you say?"

"That's right. Coker Brookstone. He died early --"

"Yes, I know. Please hold."

She sounded exhausted when she returned. "Sir? Doctor Nettleton will talk to you this afternoon. About three?"

"I'll be there," Tyler replied and took down the address.

He looked at his watch. It was a little past 11:00, and he decided to fix a quick lunch then go to the airport and see Lori. He started to back out of his driveway when something shiny caught his eye. Since it was near where Coker had fallen, he stopped to see.

As he approached, he recognized it as a chunk of the charred meteorite. It was the size and shape of a tennis ball cut in half. "The end of the meteorite," he thought aloud as he approached it. He picked the item up slowly and turned it over. The flat side was a sheer face of amber-looking glass, the same composition as the facets. The piece had apparently broken off when it was stolen! Coker must have dropped it. And Coker Brookstone had died on this spot! Being very cautious, he wrapped the object in rags and stowed it tightly in the corner of his trunk, then headed into town. He wanted to see Lori, to explain, to tell her how sorry he was for losing his temper, and tell her why the rock was so important. He stopped by the airport but Lori was not there.

Tyler found Doctor Nettleton's office and went up the stairs. After giving the receptionist his name, she immediately disappeared through a door. Tyler looked around the office then heard a door open.

Blair Nettleton was a plain-looking woman with a large mouth, thick lips and wide-set green eyes. Her hair was a silvery-blond color, and she was wearing a suit jacket and a skirt that fell gracefully to her knees. As she approached, her smile revealed sparkling white teeth. Tyler shook hands.

"About Mister Brookstone," she began, "the autopsy showed that he died by electrocution. My guess is a power line fell on him, something like that. Is that what you wanted to know?"

"Electrocution?" Tyler echoed, his hand going immediately to his head to begin scratching. "That's strange."

"Those are the findings of the forensic team, Mister Bridges. I don't know how or why, but that's what happened."

Tyler began to speak then closed his mouth. "Thank you Doctor. He died at the far end of my driveway, and I was just curious."

At Tyler turned to leave, the doctor added: "There was one thing rather strange, though."

"Oh, what's that?"

"He also showed signs of a hemorrhage in his chest."

Tyler looked at the doctor, waiting.

"There was blood all over his chest. He had bled through the skin around his heart, his carotid arteries, lungs, everything in that area. Very strange, indeed. My only guess is that he had been taking something that thinned his blood."

Tyler nodded. "I'm sure that was it, Doctor. Thank you."

-8-

On Wednesday morning, Tyler drove back to the airport and was shocked to hear from one of the line boys that Lori had called in sick and wouldn't be in the office until further notice. Tyler became worried, since she showed no sign of sickness the day before. Maybe she had just decided to stay with her father until he healed.

There was no answer at the Dennison house, so Tyler hung around the airport, hoping Lori would show up. He finally had a sandwich at the airport restaurant and was nursing a cup of coffee when he saw her car. Tossing some money on the table, he left.

Lori had just gone in her office when he drove up. When he opened the door, she looked at him, and his shock was obvious. Normally the woman wore very little makeup, but her face was dry, pale and blotchy, her eyes bloodshot and weak. That she had been crying was obvious. Tyler suddenly felt sorry for this woman who had always been so strong.

She turned quickly away from him. "Please go away," she pleaded softly.

"Look, Lori, I'm sorry --"

"I know you hated him . . . especially when he stole your . . . rock, but . . . to kill him!" She covered her face with her hands and sobbed.

Tyler stood frozen, his jaw agape. "Kill him? I didn't kill him – he swore at me when --"

"Just . . .get out!" she yelled.

Tyler backed away, feeling that his presence might bring on hysteria. A pleading look, the strained desperation in his face, the words whispered, all fell on deaf ears and blind eyes. Lori had turned with her back to him and sobbed. Tyler softly closed the door and walked slowly to the car.

On his way home, he picked up a paper and looked at the headlines. Another wave of shock hit him as he read it.

LOCAL MAN KILLED

Reid Dennison, 51, of Beverly, was killed last night near Mike's HotSpot in Beverly. Police say he was killed sometime between 11 P.M. and 1A.M. According to the police report, the victim was on his way to his car when he was shot. No further details are available.

Tyler put the paper down and drove home, saddened not for Reid Dennison but for Lori. That she actually thought he would or could do such a thing had shaken him considerably. The fact that Dennison died by violence was not in itself a surprise to Tyler, for the man's life was fraught with risk. He associated with seedy types and was frequently linked with local robberies, though he had not been convicted of any.

Tired as he was, his mind returned to thinking about his financial situation, since there was very little at the moment he could do about Reid's death or Lori's hatred of him. It was time to find out what happened to his meteorite, and why Gerald Franks was involved.

Inquiring at the university where he and Franks had attended, he was told that the last known address was the Jet Propulsion Laboratories in California. Tyler was aware of his employment there, and of his short tenure.

Tyler went through his notebooks, looking for old friends and the places they frequented. After an hour of learning nothing, he hung up the receiver and took his position in the easy chair, legs over the arm, and his hand scratching his head.

Gerald Franks was a brilliant student, an excellent roommate, and a good friend. Tyler had called him his mentor, and gave credit for his high grade average to the little guy. They had kept in touch until he left JPL in California.

During their roommate days, Tyler learned a lot about cryptology from Franks, more than he really wanted to know, mainly because language code was Gerald's passionate hobby. He had subscribed to a publication called Cryptology Monthly, or something like that. It was a magazine written entirely in code, and when it arrived, Gerald would snarl, pull his hair, fill the room with obscenities, and stomp around in the wee hours until he decrypted it. When he had solved it completely he would read the articles aloud to Tyler, wallowing in his success.

Once, Tyler asked if there was a personal code that absolutely could not be broken. Gerald laughed. "OK, let's say you and someone devise a code based on the words in a book. You know, make a digital code to show page number, line number, word number, like that."

"How would you possibly break that," Tyler asked, fearing the answer would be a simple one, making him look like a naive idiot.

"Well," Gerald said, stroking his chin, "I could easily determine that you were using that type of code by the number patterns. All I would need to find out is what book you were using."

Tyler gave him a challenging look.

"Let's see. You're a college student, so I would check your normal textbooks, since that would be easiest. If that failed, I would find out what kind of books you read for pleasure, and go through them. In your case, since I know you so well, it would be easy." Gerald lay back on his cot and smiled confidently. "Take me a couple of hours," he stated with the confidence of a boxing champion.

"OK," Tyler pursued, "What if two people would secretly get together, decide on some book that neither of them could be linked to, and make their code from that – then what would you do?"

"Ah, mosquito, you have found the Achilles heel of code breaking. That, my friend, would be a very hard code to break. By that I mean it would take a very long time, especially if you doctored it with some insignificant words and patterns."

During one of their final days of college, the two were in the library's stacks, and decided to randomly select a book they would use if they ever needed to write a code. After that, and since graduation was upon them, the subject of code breaking was never broached.

Tyler smiled at the thought. He unlimbered his long legs and headed for the kitchen when the phone rang.

"Ty? This is Gerald. Gerald Franks."

Tyler was pleasantly surprised at his good luck, and the two quickly fell into the usual questions about how things were going and who was married. When all that was concluded, Tyler's voice turned serious. "Jer? I need to talk to you about – the meteorite."

The phone went silent for a few seconds. "The meteorite? Wow. What's your link in this, Ty?"

Tyler told him of his relationship with Dennison's daughter, and the unscrupulousness of her father.

"Were those her footprints at the site?"

"Yes. And did you know you bought a piece of stolen property?"

"No, I didn't realize that, Tyler. You're saying that the meteorite is yours?"

Tyler told him of their excursion, finding the stone, and the theft from his shed by Lori's father. He explained that he knew Dennison had stolen it and confronted him, and managed to get Gerald's name, but no address. He added that Dennison had been killed.

"You didn't have anything to do with that, did you, Jer?" Tyler asked.

"Oh, God no. Why would you think that?"

"No reason," Tyler answered. "Just wondering. Tell me where you live and I'll come get my rock. I'll even reimburse you, if you want. But I need that rock, Jer," he emphasized the word need.

Tyler explained the importance of the stone due to his financial situation. Gerald listened patiently. "Tyler, I hate to tell you this, but I don't have it. Look, I would like to come see you, how about it? Maybe we can come up with a solution. OK?"

Tyler recalled how resourceful this man could be, and how solution oriented he was. "Sure, man, it'll be like old times."

They agreed on a Saturday meeting. Tyler hung up and went to the kitchen, still worried, but rays of optimism filtered through his depression. After another meal consisting of a sandwich and coffee, he once again hit his textbooks, finding hopeful relief in them.

On Thursday morning as Tyler stepped outside, a young man in a business suit stepped across the yard. "Are you Tyler Bridges?"

Tyler acknowledged and watched as he approached. The man was shorter than Tyler, but had a look of solid physical shape with a barrel chest and narrow hips. His light blue eyes scrutinized Tyler. He produced a wallet with a badge, then smiled slightly. "Sergeant Leonard Burke, Elkins State Police. I'm looking into the death of Reid Dennison. I understand you knew him?"

Tyler invited the policeman inside and nodded to a chair. "Yes. I knew him vaguely, mainly through his daughter."

"I understand you had a – a rather physical argument with him on Tuesday, the day before he was murdered."

"That's right. I accused him of trying to steal something from me and things turned a bit ugly, I'm afraid."

"Tell me about it, please."

Tyler related the events as accurately and as thoroughly as he could, without mentioning the meteorite. He just said he suspected Reid Dennison of snooping around his property, looking for something to steal. He told the officer of firing the shotgun in the air to scare them off, and about Coker collapsing.

Producing a notebook while listening, the police sergeant flipped a couple of pages, then asked: "Where were you Wednesday morning between the hours of one and three?"

Tyler grimaced. "I was here. Went to bed early after studying a while."

Officer Burke looked around, settling his gaze on the pile of chemistry books beside Tyler's chair. "Those?"

Tyler nodded.

"Tell me, Mister Bridges, do you own a gun? I mean, other than a shotgun?"

"Yes. I have a thirty-eight special that I sometimes carry in my work. You see, my job takes me in the woods and I carry it for protection."

"You have a permit?"

"Of course." Tyler walked to a cabinet and returned with a folded piece of paper, and the gun. He handed them both to the officer, who verified that the gun was not loaded. He glanced at the paper.

"I'll take the revolver. It will be returned to you after ballistics checks it."

After the officer left, Tyler spent the rest of the day working around the property. He raked leaves and trimmed shrubbery, all of which was designed to keep his mind off Lori. Losing her was not only emotionally traumatic, but also he had lost a good friend, and was now minus one charter service. That would not endear him with his employer, so Tyler decided to talk to Lori -- if she would listen -- and try to salvage at least their business relationship. This would be a difficult task at best, since she had obviously told the police about the fight with her father. It was apparent that she fully believed that Tyler had killed the old man.

Tyler leaned on his rake, his mind wandering after settling on a single fact: Things would probably never be the same between them again.

-9-

On his way to the airport on Thursday, Tyler struggled with himself as to whether he should try to talk to Lori, figuring he might make things worse, since it was so close to her father's death, or to wait. Since he really needed the charter service, he decided to try.

When he arrived, her hangar door was open and the Cessna was inside. Tyler felt a rush, a feeling of gladness that she was here, but a fear of facing her and of the outcome of their meeting.

Lori's office door was open. Tyler stood outside a moment before walking to her door and tapping lightly.

Lori turned and quickly looked away and began shuffling papers. "What do you want?"

"How are you, Lori?"

She ignored his question and continued working. "Please leave."

"I came to ask you if you would continue to be our charter service. I, we . . . need the service."

When Lori looked at him, her eyes were glassy and her expression one of condemnation, sadness and pity. "I guess," she said, fussing with a stack of papers, "that we can arrange something. I'll get someone to fly you, and I will provide the plane. Your charter will depend on the plane's availability, though. That's the best I can do."

"Well, at least that'll get me off the hook with my bosses. The police were out to see me this morning. I suppose I'm a suspect, but I would never --"

"I'll have the pilot get in touch with you," she snapped. "Now, please leave." She quickly turned her chair away.

Tyler thanked her, took a deep breath, and decided there was nothing else to say. He silently turned and walked away.

On the drive back to his house, the feeling of loneliness and abandonment fell upon him like a blanket. At home, he once again took to his textbooks to free himself from these thoughts. Alternating between studying and working around the house, Tyler managed to fill his time and divert his negative thoughts until bedtime. He climbed to the loft, turned out the light, and tried to sleep. Visions of Coker collapsing in his driveway, Dennison's bleeding face, and the shocked look on Lori's face kept invading his thoughts, delaying his sleep. He flopped, turned and fought the covers until the early morning hours of Friday before finally drifting off. The distant rumbling of thunder vibrated the windows and the wind nudged the tall trees outside.

Most of the day Friday, a light, cold rain tapped the leaves in Tyler' front yard and ticked the windows above the living room. With the exception of a quick lunch at a nearby restaurant, Tyler stayed inside. It was warm and cozy there, and gave him the chance to study and listen to music. His low mood had raised somewhat, but his vacuous feeling caused by Lori's rejection remained.

Saturday morning was bright and cold and by the time Gerald Franks stopped his sports car alongside Tyler's house, the sun was well up and illuminating the tops of the trees to the east.

After shaking hands and hugging, the two men went inside. Tyler's spirits were high. He hung up Gerald's coat and hat and began going through all the social pleasures of a conversation between friends who hadn't seen each other in almost 10 years.

Tyler poured the coffee. "So, you're working at Green Bank. I wish I had known you were so close. We could've gotten together sooner."

"Yeah. Lost touch, as they say. I've been there two, three years or so. I've meant to look you up, but, you know how it is."

"Where were you before Green Bank?" Tyler asked.

"There's a company west of here called Rossiter Dynamics. Near Flatwoods. I kinda' work for them, too, but it's a little complicated." Gerald shrugged.

"If you think it's complicated, I probably wouldn't understand any of it," Tyler conceded.

Franks suddenly looked at Tyler. "So what's up with the meteorite. It's yours, you say?"

"Sure is. Well, mine and a couple of friends who helped me find it."

"So, you want to sell it or what?" Gerald asked, pouring his cup full.

"Well, Jer, as I told you, my financial situation is in dire straights, real serious. I won't go into the gory details, only to say that I hoped to sell the meteorite, and maybe even do a write up for a magazine to help me out – how much did you pay Dennison for it?"

"Three thousand."

Tyler sank deeper into the chair, feeling the veil of despair descending upon him. He tried to keep the desperation out of his voice. "You told me you didn't have it. Where is it?"

Gerald helped himself to more coffee, then sat down. "I told you I worked at Green Bank Observatory, right? Well, I do, but I also work for Rossiter Dynamics. I told you it was complicated."

"OK, Jer, it's time for you and me to come up with something to get me some money. And I don't mean a loan."

Gerald sighed. "OK. Maybe I should tell you about Rossiter. I might have some good news for you. A guy named Kyle Rossiter owns Rossiter Dynamics, and he is working on some secret industrial project. I know a little about it, but not much, just that it has to do with something called suspension."

"Suspension? What's that mean?"

"I don't know. Anyway, I worked for him at the plant for a while. You know, engineering and stuff, and he suddenly got me a job at Green Bank. I think he felt that I was finding out too much about the project. Anyway I went to work at the observatory in some entry level position, and he paid me a retainer to supplement my salary. My only responsibility was to know when meteors landed, and get their coordinates."

"And when my, our, meteorite landed?" Tyler said, as a statement.

"Rossiter called me immediately and told me to find it pronto. I went there, and you know the rest."

"Why does he want little pieces of charred rock so badly?"

Gerald smiled. "Not all of them, just the unstable ones."

"What the hell are you talking about, Gerald?" Tyler's face twisted in confusion and anticipation.

Gerald rubbed his forehead then swept his hair back. He glanced at Tyler. "Ty, you ever hear the term single sideband?"

"Vaguely. Something to do with radio, isn't it? But, what's that got to do with --"

"Hang tight, friend," he stated patiently. "It's the only way I can explain it to you so you'll accept it." He sat on the edge of his chair. "Nearly all radio transmissions have a carrier. The information, music or talk, is in small sections called sidebands. Most of the signal's power is in the carrier, very little in the sidebands. Single sideband eliminates the carrier, therefore more power is available for the information. As an example, a twelve watt sideband signal is equal to a one hundred watt carrier signal."

"So how is the information extracted?"

"Simple. A carrier is injected at the receiver, and then it is treated just like it had a carrier all along. Genius, huh?"

"Again I ask. What does this have to do with my rock?"

"Your rock, as you call it, has a very interesting property. It is a property that I figured out when I was at Rossiter Dynamics, the one for which I got moved quickly to Green Bank."

"I must say that this is getting interesting, Gerald."

"Wait 'till you hear this. Now, as a chemist you know that the nucleus of an atom has a gazillion times more mass than the electrons surrounding it, right? Kinda' like a few specks of dust orbiting a softball. Now a hydrogen atom has one electron in orbit and it is much lighter than air. Right?"

Tyler nodded. "Tell me something I don't know, Jer."

"Well, buddy, what I am about to tell you is going to blow your mind. A couple of the meteorites that have landed have a very interesting characteristic."

"Still waiting."

Gerald looked around the room as though making sure no one was within earshot. "Their nuclei are unstable, wobbly, so to speak, and when agitated, each nucleus affected sheds its electrons – and they stay in their orbits! It's like removing our sun and the planets continue to circle around nothing!"

Tyler turned a sideways look. "What you're saying is that we have atoms with no nuclei? Atoms with . . . no mass?"

"Virtually zero."

Tyler's eyes sparkled. "So the atom suddenly becomes lighter than air!"

Gerald nodded slowly. "About 10 billion times lighter than air. When released, these atoms shoot upward until their orbits disintegrate, which is only a second or two. And, Rossiter has found a way to capture them on their way up. And that's when I was quickly booted out of Rossiter Dynamics."

Both men sat back as though exhausted. No one said anything for a few moments. Finally Tyler broke the silence.

"You said you had some good news for me."

"Oh. Right. I almost forgot. I told Rossiter about your financial situation, or what I knew of it, and that the meteorite was officially yours. I told him I thought he should compensate you for it."

"And?"

"Surprisingly, he agreed, and asked me to bring you to the plant. I think he wants to make it up to you."

Seeing the skeptical look on Tyler's face, Gerald went on: "I think he wants to make sure you're satisfied with the deal. I don't believe he wants some disgruntled guy out there talking about this special meteorite and maybe accusing Rossiter Dynamics of unfair treatment or cheating, things like that. He doesn't need the publicity, especially on the subject of meteorites."

"Well, I can understand that," Tyler agreed while pouring himself coffee. "Most companies don't want bad publicity. Do you think he will buy it from me?"

"I do. I couldn't make a guess as to how much, but I expect you'll be pleased. Rossiter is a millionaire. He has some patents on automobile computers and the software. I wouldn't worry about him haggling with you over a few dollars."

"That is good news, Jer. I'm grateful to you. When do we go?"

"When I get home, I'll call him, tell him you've agreed, and we'll set it up. I'll let you know. And, by the way, don't let on that you know anything about what I just told you. OK?"

"OK."

Tyler's woes seemed to evaporate as the weight was lifted from his shoulders. This would solve his immediate problems. Any reasonable sum would probably pay enough on the notes to hold off the bank for a few months. He told Gerald as much, and offered to buy dinner before he returned home.

Their college days, from freshman pranks to wading through the math and technologies of their senior year, to the months following graduation, all were the topics of discussion before, during and after dinner.

Tyler waved appreciatively as Gerald's sports car disappeared from sight.

Even though Gerald had brought good news, Tyler's feeling of trepidation wouldn't go away. He had known Gerald as a roommate, a friend, and mentor, and had never known him to lie, yet something did not seem right. For some unknown reason, Gerald Franks was scared.

Driving home, Gerald fought his feelings of remorse about bringing Tyler into this. Dealing with Rossiter had become unpleasant to say the least. Lately, Rossiter's anger was easily triggered, and he seemed to be suffering from paranoia. When he talked to Rossiter and suggested he compensate Tyler, the old man got mad, then cooled off. He finally conceded Gerald's plan, but warned that neither Gerald's nor his friend's life was worth anything if things did not go according to plan.

Gerald also regretted telling Tyler about the unusual properties of the meteorite. If Rossiter ever found out that Tyler knew or even suspected --.

-10-

On Monday morning Tyler was notified by the police on the results of the ballistics tests; the gun was not used in the killing of Reid Dennison, and he could pick it up at police headquarters anytime.

Later, Tyler called the police station and asked to speak to Sergeant Burke. When he came on the line, Tyler asked him if there were any developments in the case.

"We have a couple of suspects, but that is all I can say at this time."

Tyler thanked him and hung up, encouraged with what could be considered a tidbit of good news. At least the investigation had not stalled. Finding the murderer was crucial to Tyler, as Lori would never forgive him and would always think he killed her father if the real murderer wasn't found and convicted. While Tyler had put off marrying Lori, to think that his feelings for her were not strong or that their relationship could not advance was to ignore the truth.

Just before noon Gerald called with the details of their upcoming meeting with Kyle Rossiter. "I'll pick you up tomorrow morning if you can get off work."

Tyler told him that would be no problem.

"Good. I'll pick you up about nine. That should put us in Flatwoods by ten-thirty or so, and at the plant by eleven."

Fighting temptation to visit Lori and tell her about his gun, Tyler spent the rest of the day working in the yard, raking and bagging leaves.

Tuesday was another blue sky fall day with a few puffs of cumulous clouds and a white sheen of high stratus overhead. A brisk wind was streaming over the Appalachians, and Tyler flipped up his collar as he trotted to Gerald's car.

Gerald's estimate was accurate, no doubt due to the many trips he had made between Green Bank and Flatwoods, and soon they slid down the ramp at Interstate 79's exit 67. Route 15 turned south and ran parallel to the interstate for a few miles, then turned east to ride the mountaintops, when if followed far enough, would pass by where the meteorite had landed. After a short distance, however, Gerald turned onto a narrow road that climbed steadily upward past fields and houses until they could see the interstate far below.

"An airport?" Tyler blurted out as he mentally calculated that the asphalt strip they were passing was about 2000 feet long. Gerald concurred. "There's a prison near here," he added, shrugging.

At the top they wound across a plateau of fields as far as the eye could see, flatlands consisting mostly of tall grass, some orchards, and a few stands of trees.

Rossiter Dynamics, Incorporated was housed in a tall, one-story block building with a flat roof and vertical vinyl panels across most of the front. From the large parking lot one could estimate the structure to fit nicely inside the goal posts of a football field. The depth was hard to estimate, but Tyler calculated it at about half the length. "Must be at least fifty-thousand square feet," Tyler commented.

Windows along the front looked into offices, and a small section near one end had cut stone covering the front and around the end. The two men headed for the doorway with the stone facade.

Inside was everything the outside was not; the walls were light and smoothly plastered. The furniture was mahogany. There was a leather couch along the front window, and a plush chair facing it across a glass-top coffee table. An illuminated fish tank with various species spurting around graced the rear. Various diplomas and certificates dotted the walls, and a computer station jutted from the near wall. Soft music permeated the area.

The receptionist looked up from the computer screen, recognized Gerald and nodded to Tyler as he was introduced. "I'll tell Mister Rossiter you are here," she said turning, then gracefully disappeared through a rear door.

Kyle Rossiter was a large man, with a full head of light brown hair sweeping across his forehead, coiffured expertly. His handshake was a grip of steel, and his smile was cautious. His brown eyes offered no path to his feelings or his soul. He greeted Tyler in a friendly voice and invited them to his inner office.

Gesturing his guests to sit, and taking his seat behind the large desk, he leaned forward, his fingers forming a pyramid.

"Now, Mister Bridges, Gerald tells me you have been put out and have suffered some financial losses with respect to the meteorite you found."

"Call me Tyler, sir. And, yes, I went to considerable trouble to get the rock, and had plans to sell it. My financial situation is rather critical at the moment."

Rossiter's eyes flashed with interest. "OK. Tyler. How much do you think it's worth?"

"Well, I don't know. I do know that I need in excess of fifteen thousand dollars to hold off the wolves at my door."

Rossiter smiled, then sat back, a thoughtful look on his face. "As I told Gerald, we don't want any bad publicity. We are deep in government contracts, and they don't like to do business with companies that are, shall we say, on the front pages of newspapers with stories of cheating or persecuting employees, things of that nature. You see what I'm saying?"

"I understand fully, sir."

"Good. Now, as you may or may not know, every business goes through dry spells, periods where their cash flow is down, and their debts are at a critical point. Rossiter Dynamics is a solid company, but we are no exception. At the moment, we are experiencing a small cash flow problem ourselves. The timing is not the best, but I think I can come up with a solution that will be agreeable to both parties."

"Great!" Tyler blurted out, then sank in the chair as to duck the embarrassment of sounding like a boy just handed a new, shiny baseball glove.

"Here's what I propose," Rossiter said, clasping his fingers. "The stone is valuable to us, Tyler, and we have already, uh, processed some of it, so I can't return it. Therefore, here's what we'll do: I will give you five-thousand dollars cash now, which should relieve your debts momentarily, then I will issue you five-hundred shares of stock in Rossiter Dynamics. Our stock is now valued at forty dollars a share. You, of course, cannot cash them in. You can take the dividends each quarter, or you can buy more shares. How's that sound?"

Tyler's expression was one of complete surprise and pleasure.

"Oh, and anytime you want to, you can talk to our vice president and operations manager, Craig Lynch. Craig has run Rossiter Dynamics for many years, and our stockholders have long benefited from his superb performance and his business acumen. Feel free to contact him anytime. Do we have a deal?"

"Absolutely," Tyler said, rising. He shook hands with with the older man vigorously. Rossiter smiled briefly. "I'll have my secretary cut you a check. . . we'll call you a consultant, and the money and shares of stock is your payment. OK?"

"Wonderful. And thanks."

"Now," Rossiter said, with a forced smile, "why doesn't Gerald give you a tour since he is familiar with our Plant."

Gerald looked glum throughout the meeting, but perked up as he led Tyler through the reception area and down a hallway to the right. They passed offices and a few large rooms with cubicles, all showing computers. Finally they opened a door that led to the manufacturing area.

Tyler looked around, his mouth agape, eyes wide, and neck straining. The room was huge, with rows of fluorescent lights pouring brightness over the workstations, various large cabinets that housed equipment, parts and machinery. Yellow lines on the floor guided the two men between and around all the areas, finally ending in the back at a small cafeteria where a few workers were having a coffee break.

The atmosphere was courteous, cordial, and generally happy. Those working side to side seemed totally contented with what they were doing. Tyler remarked as such to Gerald. "Yes, it would seem so," he answered in noncommittal fashion.

They returned to pick up Tyler's check and headed out. Once away from the building, Gerald hurried Tyler to the car.

"If you notice, we didn't see the basement area. It's as big as the upstairs. I'm not supposed to know about that, but I discovered it by accident one night after work. I had a look around, and that's when I became suspicious about the project down there."

"Who works on the project?"

"Just Rossiter. He alone is trying to break the secret of the unstable meteorites. I'm not sure even Lynch knows about it. He uses his own money, I think, so nothing ever shows up on the books. I don't think anybody else even knows it's there."

"So you think he is somehow harnessing this . . .this lighter than air phenomenon?"

"Yes. He's developed a material that will not allow the electrons to pass, therefore creating lift. As to how much lift and for how long, I don't know. My main concern is my suspicion that he may be dealing with some unsavory characters." He glanced in the rear-view mirror. "And not just any unsavory characters, but ones from other countries."

"Hell, Jer, the way I've heard you talk about the United States, I'm surprised you're not helping him."

"What? You think that just because I cuss these crooked politicians and think that the government screws up everything it touches, that I don't love this country?"

Tyler smirked. "Well, the thought did occur to me a few years ago, based on some of our arguments."

Gerald proceeded to explain about his feelings, that he loved capitalism, the American Dream, and that he honestly grieved for those who lost their lives fighting for the freedoms they believed in. His hatred for the government was in fact due to the direction the government was headed and what it would do to the people, the economy, the dream and the memory.

As they returned to Elkins, Gerald continued to reveal what he knew about Rossiter's activities and speculating on what the options were. Tyler marveled at Gerald's intellect, wishing they could be working together as they did many years ago. Compromising, they decided to keep in touch from this day forward.

At the house, Tyler waved at the receding car and headed for the porch. Once again that forlorn feeling came over him as he ducked his head and stepped inside.

-11-

When he climbed out of bed on Wednesday, Tyler refused to let the cloudy day dampen his spirits. As though to confirm that yesterday was not a dream, he slipped downstairs and picked up the check from the table and stared at it. Having this in his hands and expecting the stock paperwork to arrive in two days gave Tyler a sense of security he had not experienced for quite a while. He whistled all the way to his newspaper receptacle, stuffed the twice-weekly publication under his arm, and gathered his mail from yesterday.

With his cup of coffee, he slumped in the chair and flipped the paper open. He jumped up, almost spilling his coffee, and stared at the headlines.

MAN ARRESTED AND CHARGED IN THE DEATH OF REID DENNISON

The article went on to explain that a cousin of Coker Brookstone, who apparently held Reid Dennison responsible for Coker's death, had confessed to the crime. He told police that he was at the bar that night, and accused Reid, who laughed in his face. Later he said, he caught Reid outside and shot him.

Tyler placed the paper down slowly, as though afraid the headlines would slide off the page. He walked to the window with his coffee and stared out onto the yard. He felt an exhilaration that had evaded him for many days. His financial obligations would be met, initially, any way, and his dividends from Rossiter would allow him extra latitude for his Mom's care, and he was free from any accusation about Reid Dennison's death.

Dismissing his first instinct to rush to Lori, he decided to retrieve his revolver from the police, then go to work. His decision to wait until tomorrow to talk to her would give her time to rearrange her feelings and to become acclimated to the idea that Tyler had nothing to do with her father's death. The time would also help to fade her mental image of Tyler's fight with him.

When he got home from work, his answering machine was blinking. Gerald had called and his voice sounded strained and hurried. "Ty, there's things developing at Rossiter's, so I may take a sabbatical for a few days. You know, get away from it all, that sort of thing. I'll call you when I get back."

The message disturbed Tyler. That things were happening at Rossiter's added to Tyler's suspicion that something was wrong, that Gerald was being less than truthful and that he was scared.

On Thursday morning, it had started to snow, and by the time Tyler had breakfasted on coffee and toast, dressed with a more than usual interest, and stepped outside, the ground was white. Tyler looked pleased as he backed out of the driveway, a hopeful look that Lori wouldn't have any charters that day.

With each mile nearer the airport, Tyler' excitement stepped up a notch, and by the time he drove up to her hangar, his heart was pounding like a teenager's at the prom. He sat in the car until his pulse slowed and his nervousness abated. Only when he felt that he could walk steadily and that his voice sounded halfway normal did he climb out and enter the hangar.

Lori was dressed in her casual outfit, the ones she usually wore on Friday if she didn't have a charter. Jeans, tight enough to show her curves, and a snug purple turtleneck sweater that would make it hard to concentrate. She sat, deep in thought until she looked up. Her eyes widened, and she immediately felt a flush in her cheeks. She stood as Tyler approached. She spoke his name and dropped her eyes, somewhat embarrassed.

"Hello, Lori. How are you?"

"Better . . .now, Ty. I guess I owe you --"

"You don't owe me anything. Your father's death was a terrible, traumatic shock to you, and I can't blame you for thinking as you did, nor should you."

Lori smiled sadly. "I know, but I should have had more faith in you, Ty. Maybe I didn't love you as much as I thought. Maybe you were right when you said I was persistent about marriage just to get away from my . . . father."

"I guess we've both had a chance to stand back and look at our relationship, and maybe it wasn't what we thought it was."

"Maybe not," she agreed, "when I look at you I still see my bleeding father on the floor and you screaming at him."

"For that I am very sorry. I lost my head that night. I guess all my frustrations about you, us, your father, all came to a head – and I shouldn't have accused him in front of you, either. No one likes to hear their father accused of being a thief."

She walked to a cabinet and opened it. "I think this is yours." She turned and extended a sheaf of bills toward Tyler. "I found this among his belongings. Take it."

"Oh, Lori, that's not really nec --"

"I want you to have it Ty. After all, the meteorite is yours, and --"

Tyler took the bills, counted out a few and tossed them on the desk. "The meteorite is *ours*, remember. You, me, and Barry. That's one thousand apiece."

Lori laughed sarcastically. "Most of this is my fault, Ty. I found my business card among Dad's things. I must have dropped it when I fell. Otherwise, there wouldn't have been a buyer and . . . none . . .of this . . . would've happened."

Tyler watched the tears beginning to build and fought the urge to take her in his arms. Instead, he clasped his hands in emphasis. "Tell you what. Let's forget about all this, put it out of our minds. Turns out that the buyer was an old friend of mine and we've renewed our friendship."

Hoping to divert her away from her thoughts, Tyler told her about Gerald Franks and his history with Rossiter Dynamics, and all the details about the financial arrangement that Rossiter had mentioned. He told her all about his former financial situation, and how his windfall money would alleviate it. Seeing her curious look, he apologized for not telling her earlier, saying he didn't want her pitying him and insisting that he take a loan from her. Listening, Lori seemed pleased, wiped her nose, and walked with him to his car. Tyler turned to her. "Maybe we could kind of start over, Lori." He watched her eyes. "Maybe you could start flying my charters again?"

Lori took a deep breath and her eyes twinkled. "You made me mad and you made me sad. I despised you for a while, maybe even disliked you for a few days. But I never stopped loving you!"

Tyler started to tell her of his feelings of abandonment and loneliness when she put a finger against his lips. "Shut up and kiss me!"

After that things were back to normal. Lori began flying the charters with him, complete with sandwiches at their destination. As winter fell with full force the river landings ended and Lori took the role of passenger in Tyler's four-wheeler. His work took them tramping along the snowy riverbanks and forests and the two used the cold as an excuse to cuddle.

Her charter service through the winter months was mainly flying a few businessmen to Charleston and Huntington, and flying medical supplies for emergency services. She also secured a few contracts with photographers to take pictures of the winter scenery along the Appalachians.

Lori spoke rarely of her father. Tyler had undertaken the role of mentor and insisted she visit her father's grave frequently, and to think and talk only about the good times. Lori's love for Tyler grew as the winter months passed. Since she had no family, she accepted Tyler's invitation to stay with him through the Thanksgiving and Christmas holidays. They roamed the woods, had snowball fights, and went sled riding in the daytime and snuggled together in his loft at night.

Lori loved her house, too, and used her extra time to remodel and redecorate. She and Tyler had friends in for parties and various functions, which revolved mostly around Tyler's animal shelter fund raising, and the Meals on Wheels program.

As green replaced the white on the ground and warmer water flushed the ice from the rivers and lakes, the two lovers once again resumed their jaunts in the air.

"When am I going to meet Gerald," Lori asked one spring afternoon while they were aloft.

"Well, now that good weather is here, I'll call him and invite him over, how's that?"

"Great. He can sleep at my house," she said as she leaned over and nibbled his ear then giggled. "That way, we won't keep him awake."

During the first week of April, Tyler decided to invite Gerald for the weekend. He had talked to him only twice over the course of the winter, and as Tyler recalled, the last time he sounded troubled. When he told Lori about it, she agreed that the respite would do him good.

Tyler tried three times on Monday, April 2, but could not reach him. He put the phone down slowly and stared outside.

Something was wrong.

Gerald's calls had stopped, and now the inability to reach him was beginning to pervade Tyler's mind.

Gerald's situation was replaced in Tyler's mind by the piece of meteorite broken off the original. He had brought the mysterious stone inside and had carefully put it on the table, flat side down.

Head resting on his knuckles, he studied it at length, the conical shape broken by the still fascinating facets gleaming in the overhead light. He drew a quick breath as one might do when about to dive underwater. He extended his arm to the stone, and, with a table knife, scraped the amber glass.

A bulb in the overhead light exploded, and the entire fixture wobbled. Tyler ducked instinctively then looked up, fascination showing in his eyes.

He had released the electrons!

They had shot upward and broken the vacuum of the bulb, then had passed through the fixture, probably through the roof, although there were no signs of any holes. Tyler laughed at his ignorance. Electrons are too small to leave holes in wood! But these weren't just electrons. They were actually atoms with no centers!

A few seconds passed before the magnitude of what had just happened settled in Tyler's brain. A simple scratch had started a force powerful enough to kill a man, or maybe propel something into space, or maybe --

Tyler shook the thoughts away and looked up as Lori came in. "Want to see something interesting?" he asked as she headed for the coffeepot. "Sure, what is it?"

He sat her down, made her sit back, and scratched the glass as he had done before. The second light bulb popped and Lori yelped, her hand coming to her mouth, her eyes wide and unblinking. "What the hell was that?" she asked, breathless.

"I'm still trying to figure out if this just happened." Tyler answered.

As both sat in shock and stared, the telephone rang. Finally Tyler got up and answered it. He listened a moment, frowning, and Lori got up, sensing something was wrong.

Tyler looked at the receiver, then listened quickly once more before he replaced it.

Worried, Lori circled the table, her eyes locked on Tyler. "What is it, Ty?"

The young man looked at her, his face a mask of shock. "That was Gerald," he stated hypnotically. "He whispered 'Ty, the letter', then I heard a grunt and the line went dead."

-12-

Lori accompanied Tyler to Gerald's house for his memorial service on Wednesday. No one seemed to know exactly why he had been strangled or who had done it. Someone said they suspected robbery, but nothing was vandalized as far as anyone knew, only a thorough search of the house. Opinions were running high that there was a mentally deranged killer running around the area, a theory that Tyler instinctively and immediately dismissed. Gerald had apparently requested that he be cremated, since he had no family. His attorney had seen to the details.

The investigation was handled by the observatory's security force -- in lieu of an investigative branch of the police -- but Tyler couldn't find out any details about the murder, or anything else, for that matter. As he and Lori moved around, he didn't recognize anybody at the service. The two or three there, he figured were Gerald's co-workers. Just before they were preparing to leave, Tyler spotted Craig Lynch, whom he described to Lori as the man in charge of his new investments at Rossiter.

"Mister Bridges, isn't it?" the older man asked as they caught his attention on approach.

"Yes, sir. Gerald was an old friend of mine. We go way back to our college days."

Lynch shook his head. "Tragedy, tragedy, I say. Man's not safe even in his own house. Gerald was a nice person."

"He surely was," Tyler concurred in a broken voice. Lori squeezed his hand.

Walking to the car, Tyler asked Lori to drive. He slumped in the seat and remained quiet for most of the way back. He stared at the passing scenery until finally breaking the silence. He turned to Lori. "I wonder what he meant."

"Who?"

"Gerald. When he called me Monday night. His voice was weak. He was either whispering to keep from being heard, or he was being strangled. All he managed to say was 'The letter'."

"What letter?" Lori asked.

"That's what I've been thinking about. A letter from college? We didn't earn any."

"You write him a letter recently?"

"No."

"Maybe he wrote you one?"

Tyler sighed. "Well, if he did, I never received it. Or maybe I might get it in a day or two. If not, I'm stumped. Probably will never know."

Lori left Tyler's house after she fixed him a meal and made sure he was all right. "I would love to stay, Ty, but I have to meet some people."

Tyler encouraged her to go, pleased that she was regaining interest in her charitable activities and her life in general.

On Friday morning Tyler received a telephone call which the caller ID showed to be someone named Sidney Tarrant.

"Mister Bridges?"

"Speaking."

"My name is Sidney Tarrant. I'm a lawyer acting as executor of Gerald Frank's will. As such, I have gone through his things at the house and I came across an envelope addressed to you. It looks like it has been sealed then torn open, by whom or when I do not know. I haven't looked at the contents. Would you like me to do so now?"

Tyler could feel his pulse in his ear. "Yes, please."

Paper rattled then the voice continued. "It looks like two pages with some numbers, Mister Bridges. At the top of the first page it says, 'Today's notations and tabulations.' Nothing else, just that and then the numbers. Would you like me to send it to you?"

Tyler asked the lawyer to please do so, thanked him, and hung up. He called Lori, told her about the lawyer's find, and promised to let her know when the letter arrived.

When it came to obsessing, Tyler Bridges had no equal. Through most of the weekend, whether working, relaxing, reading or cooking, even when in the company of Lori, Tyler could not break away from studying, pondering and theorizing about the forthcoming letter. Any attempt in communication with Tyler had to be repeated as the first attempt always drew a "Huh? What?" followed by an awakening just long enough to deal with the current conversation, after which he would slide back into the recesses of his thoughts.

A few days later, the staring, frowning, grimacing and smirking preoccupation ceased momentarily as Tyler extracted the letter from his mailbox and went inside to call Lori.

As though his obsession was some contagious disease, Lori dropped what she was doing, threw on some sweats, pulled her hair back, forgot her makeup and was at his house within twenty minutes of receiving his call.

The two pages had been ripped from a spiral binder. The papers were college ruled, the first marked with a 1 in the top left corner, and a 2 in the identical location on the second. "He used to number his notes exactly like that," Tyler remarked sadly.

Lori's eyes scanned the documents busily. "Have you figured out anything yet?" she asked as her eyes floated around the page. "What's this mean 'Today's tabulations and notations'? He a bookie or something?"

"Of course not. Gerald Franks never gambled in his life, nor would he associate with anybody who did."

Lori ran her fingers across the page. "These numbers? Is this some kind of code?"

"I'm glad I took up with a smart girl. Yes, it's a code, that's for sure. It's not binary, and I don't think it's hex, but it's surely a co --"

Tyler headed for the door. "Let's go," he urged.

"Where to?"

A satisfied smile broke across his face. "The library!"

On the way into town, Tyler seemed relaxed and non-obsessive. He was happy and a bit giddy. He told her a fish joke and watched her laugh.

"Gerald would've called me an idiot, for sure," he said thoughtfully as he stared at the top page.

"Why?"

"For not seeing this code immediately. But I had forgotten about it. You see, this is a common code that any half-witted code breaker would spot in the bat of an eye."

"Simple?" she asked.

"Sure. These groups of numbers give it away. Look here," he said, pointing to the first line. "Zero-three-two, then zero-two, then zero-two. Three small groups within the main group."

Lori mimicked Tyler by scratching her head. "Still no comprehend."

"Page number, line number, word number. Page thirty-two, the second line, then the second word. Simplest code in the world to break – if you know what book it refers to!"

Suddenly he glanced at the papers she was holding and laughed. "He faked them out!" he announced proudly.

"Who faked out who -- whom?"

"That sentence at the top about notations and tabulations? It doesn't mean crap. That was Gerald's way to keep someone from figuring out it was a code! If they had, they would have destroyed it."

"OK, fine, genius. But why are we heading to the library."

"To check out a book, my dear, to check out a book."

The library was on Davis Avenue and the parking was easy, due to the hour. Darkness was falling quickly and the skies were getting cloudy. Lori and Tyler stepped inside and headed for the computer terminals.

"What are we looking for?" Lori asked, sitting down.

"Gibbons' Decline and Fall of the Roman Empire, Volume One."

"O.K.," she whispered slowly. "And just how in God's name did you get that from these pages?"

"Didn't. Gerald and I worked that out years ago."

In answer to Lori's blank, confused expression, Tyler told her of Gerald's love of cryptology and how they had devised a code based on this book."

"Why *this* book," she whispered.

"Because nobody in his right mind would think I had any interest in it. And they would be right."

"No understand again," she said, shaking her head.

"Forget it. It's a code thing. Let's go get the book."

Their search was quick but futile. Tyler soon realized that the copy was not available on the shelves, which meant he would need to ask the librarian, something he didn't want to do for fear someone – a code breaker – might trace it to him. After spouting his theory to Lori and looking at her reaction, he realized it sounded like he had dived off the deep paranoid end.

The librarian produced the book with instructions that it was not to be taken out of the reading room. The two nodded with understanding and huddled on a couch at the rear of a small room, well lighted, and quiet.

"Look at the first line, Lori, and read me the first seven digits."

Lori looked at the first few sets of numbers.

> 130 07 04 190 10 03 158
> 04 07 268 01 02 032 01 03

The digits were neatly spaced. Lori whispered the numbers as Tyler opened the book.

"One three zero zero seven zero four."

Tyler flipped the pages carefully. "Write this word down. Repentance. Next."

"One nine zero one zero zero three."

"Over," he said, watching Lori write it down.

"One five eight zero four zero seven."

"Subjects."

"Two sixty eight zero one zero two."

"Induced."

"Zero three two zero one zero three."

"They."

"One one four zero six one zero."

"Reason. Now look at the first letter of each word."

Lori read them slowly. "R O S I T R –"

"Rossiter." Tyler expounded.

After that Lori read the digits and Tyler would call out just the letter. It was slow, drudging work and the time passed slowly. The two worked diligently until the librarian stuck her head in the room and informed them that it was closing time.

A light patter of raindrops greeted the two as they headed to Tyler's car. Once inside, Lori looked at her scribbles. "So far the first page reads ROSITRNLKDAPLNFLYOVRP WRSTNXPLODSTOPHM."

Tyler laughed as Lori spluttered through the phonetic pronunciation. "We'll get the rest deciphered tomorrow, then we can try to figure out what it all means. Maybe it's just a joke."

Lori stared at her side window. "Ty? I think we're being followed."

Tyler quickly glanced in the rear-view mirror and noticed two tiny headlights in the distance. He turned at the next street and wound through a residential area before resuming his route. The headlights were gone.

"I guess I'm getting paranoid, too." Lori admitted, turning forward. "Ty?"

"Yes?"

"Can I stay with you tonight? I'm scared."

"Of all the excuses to get in my pants."

Faking a slap at him, she grabbed Tyler's arm and they went inside, too occupied with each other to notice the car slowly passing their driveway.

-13-

It rained hard during the night, one of those spring storms that left puddles scattered throughout Tyler's front yard. Distant thunder punctuated the hissing sound on the windows and raindrops pecking on the roof. By the time Tyler and Lori finally woke up, the rain had diminished, and only the dripping from the trees remained as evidence of the night's precipitant performance.

After a quick breakfast, the two returned to the library, assumed their places in the reading room, and were hunched over, totally engrossed in the process of deciphering Gerald's code.

By noon they were stiff, numb and exhausted, but decided to finish the job before going to lunch. For some reason, Tyler, for reasons he couldn't explain, felt a strong urge to complete the message.

At 1:30, they hurried to the car. Lori climbed in and scooted over, clasping the fruits of their labor to her breast.

As they navigated the city streets, Lori was looking first forward, then to the rear. She nervously checked her side mirror every few seconds.

"Still think we're being followed?" Tyler asked, glancing at her.

"Just checking, that's all."

Lori was so busy scrutinizing the people along the streets and the buildings, she was not aware of Tyler's constant glances in his rear view mirror. Only when she spoke to him and he did not answer did she notice. "What's wrong, Ty?"

"I think you were right. We *are* being followed."

Again they took a circuitous route through a residential section near Tyler's house. After their departure from a normal route, the car disappeared. Tyler watched his back trail carefully then turned in his driveway.

At Lori's insistence, Tyler locked the door and pulled the blinds over the side windows, a move that prevented him from seeing a car pass the driveway slowly.

Lori was excited and pressed out the wrinkled paper then turned it over. She had put the decoded message on the back. Both looked at the jumbled letters across the page:

ROSITRNLKDAPLNFLYOVRPWRSTNX-
PLO DSTOPHMHRDBSTOHLPUGODWNST-
PSATLNTSECODIAFDBHGONNFNDMTLBX
WNOBDSTRY...

Within the hour, Tyler had expanded the shortened text into words that made sense, and stood looking at the paragraph, his eyes darkened and his brows pulled down. He glanced over at Lori, who had fallen asleep at the table, and spoke her name.

The girl jumped as if shot then blinked the sleep out of her eyes. "Sorry, Ty. Guess things just caught up with me."

"It's OK. Just wanted you to know I've finished the text. I've written down what I think Gerald was trying to tell me."

Lori stretched. "What's it say?"

"You won't like it. Here," he handed her a piece of paper, which she began reading. Her expression changed almost immediately then she frowned.

"Read it back to me," Tyler insisted, "I want to hear it."

"OK. It says 'Rossiter is going to sell to Al Qaida devices that will fly over power stations and drop explosives.' Gerald wants you to stop them. He hired someone called BS to help. He says you should go down the steps at the plant. He says the security code is IAFDBH, which might mean 916428, their position in the alphabet. Apparently Rossiter is gone on Mondays. You are to find a metal box with a knob. He says to destroy it at all cost."

Lori was stunned. She put the paper down. "We've got to tell the police about this."

Tyler smirked. "Tell them what? That a friend of mine was strangled as he talked to me on the telephone, and that he believes little men on flying platforms are going to drop bombs on all the power plants across the country? Hell, they'd take me to the funny farm!"

"What are you going to do? And who is BS?"

"The first thing I'm going to do is find out who is following us."

Somehow Tyler did not believe the person following them meant harm, or he would have moved accordingly. Perhaps he was just tracking their movements, Tyler said, thinking aloud. In any event, he didn't want to involve Lori in case there was trouble. When he made her aware of his decision, her blue eyes turned hard and she placed her hands on her hips and stood in front of him defiantly.

"Tyler Bridges, I didn't become a pilot to hide from danger, nor did I tromp around with you in snake-infested riverbanks because I was looking for a safe place to walk! I'll be damned if you're going off on some caper like James Bond without me!"

Tyler placed his hands, palms outward, in front of him. "OK. So you go along. If you get shot full of holes don't expect me to plug them up – at least not right away."

Tyler explained his plan to find out who was following them, then climbed in the back and lay down. Lori drove and headed for the library, her instructions being that she was to notify Tyler if she spotted anyone following.

Arriving there, she went inside, and in a few minutes appeared and went to the car. Soon afterward she started toward Tyler's house, she glanced in the mirror. "There he is, back a block or so, same car as I saw yesterday."

"Can you see what he looks like?" asked the voice from the back seat.

Lori stretched her neck. "No, only that he's big or it's a woman with a lot of hair. I can't tell."

Tyler told Lori to make sure the distance was great, then pull alongside a store, get out quickly and go inside.

"Got it, Mister Bond," she quipped.

Suddenly Tyler felt the car swerve to the right and stop. He heard the door slam and Lori's steps receding. He waited a few seconds then peeked over the seat. The black car was speeding up, ready to pass. Tyler crawled to the rear passenger door, opened it, and stood up just as the car was passing.

Barry Southerland's eyes were straight ahead but he caught a glimpse of Tyler, and he knew he had been recognized. He found a place to park a couple of spaces ahead, and pulled in.

Lori caught up with Tyler just as Barry climbed out.

"Barry? What's going on?"

The big man smiled guiltily. "Well, you caught me. I've been following you."

Neither of the approaching two said anything.

"Gerald hired me to look out for you. He said you might be in danger and that I should tail you for a couple of weeks. He figured if you knew you'd call me off."

"Gerald is dead," Tyler said curtly. "Let's go back to my place where we can talk. Besides, I owe you some money."

Barry and Lori scooted chairs and sat down while Tyler went to make coffee. When he returned and sat down, Barry asked: "What the hell is going on, Ty?"

Tyler told him about Gerald's association with Rossiter Dynamics, and how he suspected that something evil was going on there. He mentioned about he himself meeting Kyle Rossiter and how things had gone financially. Lori filled him in on the letter of code they had received, and how the message was decoded. Tyler purposely left out the theft of his rock by Dennison, and the following deaths of Dennison and his accomplice Coker Brookstone.

"That accounts for the trips to the library," Barry added as Tyler got up. "So what's the message say?"

Tyler fetched the fresh coffee and poured the cups. "Gerald told us by code that Kyle Rossiter is planning on building small machines that defy gravity. He intends to sell them to terrorists. Imagine a terrorist being able to silently ride a tiny platform to any height where he could drop a bomb. This would jeopardize all our power plants, not to mention dams, bridges, substations, industrial complexes and even ships in the harbors. They could jump fences, gain access to virtually any compound such as prisons, jails, everything. It's scary, and Gerald somehow planned to stop them."

"Defy gravity?" Barry leaned his chair back and put on a look of skepticism. "Sounds like little green men from Mars, to me? You sure this isn't some kind of joke, Ty?"

Lori and Tyler looked at each other. Lori asked Barry to step away from the table as Tyler went to get the broken meteorite. "This is a piece of the meteorite we found," she explained. "Watch."

Tyler placed the object directly under a bulb, shaded his eyes and scratched the stone lightly with a fork tine. Barry jerked when the bulb popped.

"This thing releases energy, Barry. So much energy that if controlled it can lift a body, maybe even much heavier stuff. Apparently Rossiter is close to doing that."

Barry stood, mouth wide, unbelieving look in his eyes. "Wow," was all he could say.

"Good. I'm running out of light bulbs."

Having heard Tyler's commitment to somehow stop Rossiter's plan, Barry argued caution and patience, saying they would need to give a lot of thought before doing anything. This, Tyler noted, meant Barry had unconsciously included himself in the forthcoming task. Having Barry along probably meant the difference between success and failure, although Tyler had misgivings about risking someone else's life, especially a friend like Barry.

"Don't give it another thought," Barry told him when Tyler cautioned him. "If what you say is true, we don't have a choice. He has to be stopped. If it isn't true, then all we do is a little breaking and entering, no one gets hurt, and at worst we are out a little time and money. If we don't get caught, that is."

Lori listened quietly, her interest in the plan showing all over her face. "What about me?" she asked, defiantly folding her arms.

Telling her she wasn't needed would be like telling her that women should be kept barefoot and pregnant, and neither man wanted to risk the consequences of a remark like that. So she was allowed to include herself by volunteering to drive, or to provide a distraction if it became necessary.

"I'll wear a short skirt and high heels, a tight sweater and a fluffy hairdo." She put a hand to her thigh, tilted her head and raised an eyebrow.

"Just great," Tyler mumbled sourly. "My girl looks like a prostitute while I'm breaking and entering with my best friend."

After briefing Barry on the few details he had picked up at the plant, Tyler stood on the porch and watched the big man splash to his car.

Inside, Lori gathered the dishes, cleaned up and headed for home. "Some things I need to do at home, sweet. I'll see you tomorrow." She kissed his nose, pulled her sweater across her head and went through the rain. Tyler watched her from the porch, listening to the rain, and wishing she had stayed. That feeling of loneliness came over him again. He shivered and went inside.

-14-

The plan was for late Sunday night and Monday morning. Meanwhile, Lori worked her charters, one on Thursday afternoon took her to Zanesville, Ohio, and a flight Saturday morning to Huntington, both holdover flights which limited her time with Tyler. He was kept busy at the hatcheries, and had to drive to a few nearby stocking areas, too close by to justify Lori's charter service, even if they had been available.

On Saturday night, Lori met Tyler for dinner before they retreated to his house. The weather had turned cold and Lori stood shivering and rubbing her arms while Tyler started a fire.

Once the blaze had caught, the small room warmed quickly. A short time later the couple found themselves snuggled on the couch, staring into each others' eyes. Tyler told her about the strange feeling of abandonment and loneliness after she left on Wednesday, and that it had happened before, especially those days when they had stopped seeing each other. Lori straightened up quickly and stared thoughtfully at him. "Ty?"

"Yes?"

"I do believe you've just told me you love me."

Tyler looked down studiously and pursed his lips. "I don't remember saying that – but you might be right."

The loft was warm and cozy. Lori smiled contentedly as she wiggled her naked body under the covers next to Tyler. The bed was soon warmed by their lovemaking. Lori's passion found new heights, and all of Tyler's feelings of abandonment and loneliness had ceased to exist.

Outside, the cold wind blew.

On a mountaintop to the south, Barry Southerland's wife studied her husband's face. "What's wrong, Barry. You seem worried."

He had, in fact, shown a preoccupation that was only matched when he watched football or fishing programs on TV. The big man rubbed his beard. "If this flying thing is on the level, and I'll give Tyler the benefit of doubt, then I have to destroy it. Problem is, Ty may want to keep it, study it, maybe even try to fly it." Southerland's face became a mask, his eyes vacant. "I can't let him keep it. The thing *has* to be destroyed, that's all there is to it."

Robin Southerland had never seen her husband this disturbed about anything before. She watched him, a troubled look in her eyes, for a long time before finally falling to sleep.

Sunday was unseasonably cold. The icy air came sliding across the Great Lakes, made its way down through Illinois, Indiana and Ohio before picking up more chill when it entered the mountains east of the Ohio River.

Tyler and Lori slept late, enjoying the warmth and quiet of the cabin. Tyler wanted to be fully rested for the task ahead. He suddenly missed Gerald, for whom he was about to illegally enter a manufacturing plant and steal an object. It was uncanny that his friend had managed to steal the security code, without which the task would be near impossible. And with any luck, he and Barry could be in and out with no interference.

With clear skies through the day and a forecast for the same overnight, everybody was planning on a cold outing. Lori donned her coat and the others followed. By 11 P.M. they were in Tyler's car and heading west to intercept Interstate 79 at Weston. Then they headed south and Lori estimated they would be at Rossiter's a little after midnight. Traffic was light, but Tyler kept his speed within limits.

Exiting the highway at Flatwoods, Tyler pulled over and stopped. "You drive, Lori. You need to remember the road."

After directing Lori along the road leading to the plateau, Tyler remarked that he had been surprised that there was a runway here.

"Braxton County Airport," Lori told him. "I've landed here a couple of times. There's a convention center down below, and a regional prison nearby. Surprising amount of traffic for a rural airport."

The entrance to Rossiter Dynamics surprised Lori. She stared at the large, black, empty parking lot. According to Tyler's directions, she turned the car around, backed up near a stand of trees in a far corner, and turned off the lights. She took a deep breath. "Well, here we are."

"Lori, you stay here. Keep down low if you see anything," Tyler instructed.

Lori's expression couldn't be seen in the dark interior of the car, but when Tyler opened the door he noticed the sulky look she was giving him. "Sorry, honey, but I can't afford to worry about you in there."

As the two crossed the parking lot, Tyler looked back at his car, and if it hadn't been dark he would have seen Lori thumbing her nose.

Moving quickly along the front, Tyler led them along the darkened office windows to the main entrance door. After a few paces, they were moving along the side. Tyler was sneaking along the block surface, remembering that Gerald had mentioned a single door that led downstairs.

He found it around the back of the huge structure. There was a small parking lot, no doubt for Rossiter himself, and a walkway leading to a small awning over a doorway. Tyler snapped on his pencil light and found the metal box located on the side.

There were 10 buttons, labeled 1 through 9 and a 0. Tyler looked at Barry who nodded affirmatively. Tyler inhaled deeply, punched the numbers, and waited. Something inside clicked and Barry pulled the handle. The heavy metal door opened easily and smoothly.

They were in!

Gerald had mentioned that there didn't appear to be a security system, mainly because Rossiter wanted no attention called to the underground space. And since there were no accesses from the upper floor, and no windows, motion detectors or door switches were not needed. At least that was the thinking of Kyle Rossiter, according to what Gerald had told him.

Tyler flashed the beam around and found a panel of switches. He shot Barry a questioning glance and Barry shrugged. Tyler flipped a switch.

A bank of fluorescent lights flickered then came on. Both men blinked then looked around. They were in a large high-ceilinged room, with rows of workbenches, all littered with tools, electronic parts, pipes, gears, cabinets and other devices only known to Rossiter. The room resembled the large floor space of the manufacturing plant directly above. Large, gray cabinets, 8 feet high, lined one wall. Ahead, along the front of the room, there were more benches and worktables, all strewn with parts of all descriptions.

The men meandered along the tables, studying any object that they didn't recognize. Barry would point or hold something up and Tyler would nod no. They circled all the tables in the room to no avail. Nothing that looked like the box Gerald had described in the code. Finally Barry went over and flipped more light switches. More fluorescent tubes flickered, and the room became brilliant with white light. They moved to a doorway along the left wall and slid back the panel.

Another room similar to the first, lay before them. Work tables strewn about, parts everywhere. Along the rear wall there were cartons, boxes, both wooden and cardboard, standing one atop the other. Barry's interest turned to the boxes; Tyler studied various chunks of metal on the other tables.

"Looks like Rossiter's trying different metals. What's in the boxes?"

Barry moved across the front of a line of smaller cartons. "This one says Alkali Metals, another one Lanthanoids, Actinoids. Mean anything?"

"Well," Tyler said as he inspected a piece of metal he had identified as titanium, "Those are all metal and alloy families. Not what we're looking for."

Barry waved. "Hey, back here's another door."

As the panel swept back, Tyler gasped. Sitting on a table in the center was a metal box exactly as Gerald had described it. The metal had a dull, bluish color that Tyler guessed was either titanium or magnesium. Barry said, "Here's the knob you were talking about."

Tyler approached the unit slowly while looking around. Cannisters of Oxygen, Acetylene, Nitrogen, Argon and other bottles of gas were standing along one wall.

Both men studied the object on the table, walking slowly around and squatting down at times, never getting above the box.

Barry looked at Tyler. "Let's turn the knob and see what happens."

Tyler started to refuse, but changed his mind and nodded yes. Barry kept at arm's length and grabbed the small knob with two fingers and slowly turned it clockwise.

Nothing happened, so he kept turning until the knob reached its limit.

Barry's eyes turned bright. "Let's get an axe or something and smash it, Ty. It's evil!"

"Not yet, Bear. I'm going to try to get it open and take the meteorite out of it. It's worth money to us."

The big man seemed to deflate slightly. He nodded. "OK, but as soon as you do, I want to destroy it!"

Tyler picked up the box, surprised how light it was, and noticed that the top of the table was wet. "Get me that rag over there," he asked Barry. Barry tossed him the rag and he wrapped the box with it and had placed it under his arm when a movement in the doorway caught his attention.

"Hold it right there, you two!"

A uniformed security guard stood, feet planted apart, and had his pistol pointed toward Barry. "Move over close to him," he said, motioning with the pistol. Barry moved over slowly, eyes fixed on the guard. "Whatever you're carrying there, mister, put it down," he stated firmly.

Tyler laid the box, still wrapped, on the table and stepped back.

"Both of you," the guard snapped, "put your hands on your head and don't move!"

The men did as they were told and stood motionless. The guard slowly sidestepped along the wall and picked up a telephone receiver. He glanced quickly once and pressed one button. After a few seconds, he spoke. "Mister Rossiter. This is Billingsly at the plant. I was making my rounds outside when I saw a door open. I went inside and found two men trying to steal something from the basement." He listened a few seconds. "Yessir," he answered then hung up.

"You two come slowly around the table and walk toward me." As the men did what they were told, the guard backed toward the door and as he stepped through the doorway, he suddenly fell forward, his hat flew off, and he smacked the floor.

Lori stood there, a piece of wooden pallet in her hand. "So you don't want to worry about me, huh? Bet you're glad I came along now, aren't you?"

Tyler quickly went to the table, grabbed the wrapped box and said: "Let's get out of here. Rossiter's probably on his way with an army or something!"

Barry knelt down and grabbed the guard's pistol.

"He OK?" Lori queried, her face twisted.

"He's coming to now." Barry said, rising, "Let's go."

At the entrance, Tyler slammed the metal door shut and the trio ran to the car.

Driving back with Lori at the wheel, the three were silent for the first few miles. Lori glanced toward Tyler. "What happens if that guard identifies one of us."

"I've been thinking about that, too," Barry said, "but Rossiter won't tell anyone who we are and what we stole. The secret would be out. He doesn't want a newspaper getting hold of this, they might find out what he's doing. No. he will just want his machine back."

"That's what scares me a little," Tyler remarked, his face drawn into a frown. "He might try to buy it back, then again he may attempt to steal it back."

"I say we destroy it . . . now!" Barry's voice boomed.

"Not yet, Bear," Tyler said softly. "Now let's quiet down and let me think."

-15-

"Lori, you still have that old hi-fi amp?" Tyler asked after a few minutes.

"Sure, why?"

"It'll make a good decoy in case anyone wants to steal Rossiter's box."

"Then what are you going to do with it," Barry asked when they arrived at Tyler's. "I mean, we need to destroy that thing."

"Look, Bear. That rock is worth a lot of money for all three of us. Nobody destroys anything until I get the stone. And we know what the rock can do if disturbed. So I'll take my time, if you please."

In a gesture bordering on defiance, the big man finally nodded in a half-heartedly way. "Where you gonna' hide it," he asked softly.

Tyler scratched his head. "Uh, I'll put the decoy in my shed, and the real thing in Lori's garage."

As the two walked to Barry's truck, Tyler slapped him lightly on the back. "Don't worry, Bear. As soon as I extract the rock and finish my examination of the thing, you are welcome to it. Do with it what you please. I will even help. I promise. OK?"

The effect was disarming, and Barry smiled as he climbed into his truck. "Give me a call soon?"

Tyler assured him he would, and watched, troubled, until the truck had turned out of sight. Then he climbed in his car and followed Lori to her house where he wrapped the amplifier in the same rags as the meteorite box.

"Put it on the shelf over there," Tyler said, pointing.

Lori's face twisted curiously when she came back. "That ain't what you told Barry," she said melodiously.

"I know," came a musical reply. "Because I didn't like the look in his eyes. You ever see the movie Treasure of the Sierra Madres?"

"I think so. Humphrey Bogart went nuts about the gold – Oh, I get it."

"Barry is a great fishing partner, but I'm not sure I trust him. He seems mighty determined to destroy that thing. I believe he thinks it is some kind of evil spirit or something."

"So where are you going to hide it?"

"In your hangar, if that's OK."

"Sure," Lori exclaimed. "The place has a good security system. If anyone tries to jimmy a door, alarms will go off and all hell breaks loose."

Without delay, they drove to the airport, and once inside the hangar, and with the door shut and locked, the two went to Lori's office and Tyler placed the metal box on the desk. Curious, Lori watched Tyler inspect the sides, top and bottom, and ends. The single knob stood proud of the box, and, as though it was taunting him, Tyler moved back to arm's length, turned the knob slowly. Still, nothing happened, so he continued studying the device. A pipe flange was mounted in the center near one side, a connector of some sort beside it, and a cylinder about the size of a beer can protruded on the other. The bottom was sealed with the exception of a small hole near each corner. Near one side, there was a panel measuring about 5 inches by 9 inches, held tight by standard screws. Lori left and came back a few minutes later with a screwdriver. Tyler removed the screws then pried the panel open.

Both stared in awe.

Inside was the meteorite. The charred outer layer had been removed, leaving only a clear, amber quartz-like faceted material. One end had been broken or sliced off, maybe the same surface that was left when Coker dropped it that night.

"It's gorgeous!" Lori exclaimed, her hand pressing her heart. "What a beautiful piece of jewelry that would make."

"Until it killed you, of course," Tyler added.

"Ug, there is that," she agreed.

Tyler replaced the panel and screws and resumed his inspection. There were numerous screw heads protruding and Tyler looked closely at them. "Splines," he finally muttered angrily. "You have any spline wrenches around here?"

Lori stared, amusingly. "Spline wrenches? Oh, sure. Airplanes are full of spline screws."

Tyler laughed and shook his head. "Sorry. Lost my head, Amelia – let's go back to my place. I don't want you around your house tonight, in case you have visitors."

Realizing they were both famished, they delayed the trip to Tyler's long enough to eat. "I don't want fast food, Ty," Lori pleaded, so they headed for a restaurant and ate a meal. The waiter gave them a strange look when they ordered an evening menu since they were set up for breakfast. He respected their wishes and served them baked potatoes and salads for which both were grateful. They ate slowly and appreciatively, talking very little, and followed the meal with some slow conversation over coffee. Finally Tyler made scooting noises with his chair. It was 4 A.M. when they left the restaurant. Thirty minutes later, they pulled into Tyler's driveway and he immediately spotted the door to the shed standing open. "Stay here," he told Lori.

"Not on your life," she whispered, grabbing his coat tail.

As they slowly moved past the front porch, Lori tugged on Tyler's jacket. She pointed to the front door, which was standing open. Tyler, hunched, straightened up. "I guess we've had visitors. Let's look inside the shed first."

Tyler snapped on the lights, and the two stood in the doorway looking around. Nothing seemed out of order. A few items had been moved, a few things changed on the shelves, but nothing was destroyed. Tyler turned out the lights and closed the door.

At the house and with the lights on, the two stood in the doorway and stared at the carnage. The chair cushions had been split open, the stove emptied and ashes scattered on the floor, the closets ransacked. Every drawer had been opened, the contents strewn on the floor, and all the rugs had been yanked up and thrown aside.

"Oh, Tyler," Lori consoled quietly, her eyes were wide and wet.

"I guess Mister Rossiter knows who took the rock, wouldn't you say?"

Lori nodded absently.

Standing in the middle of books, magazines, papers, and dishes, Tyler scratched his head. "I don't think Rossiter did this. If he wanted the thing that badly, I think he would've used a different method."

"Like what?"

"I don't know. I just think this isn't the way Rossiter would go about it. Even though he's desperate, I think he would've talked first, maybe threatened, but talked."

"Who else?" Lori asked, tossing a bundle of papers on the table. "You don't think Barry?"

"Oh, no. Not Barry. He's a little rough around the edges, and he certainly wants to destroy the rock, but he wouldn't go this far."

For the next hour, the two gathered, sorted, stuffed, swept and cleaned. Lori looked at the light from the east. "Maybe I better check my house and garage."

Lori waited in the car until Tyler returned from the shed, stuffing something in his pocket. "Let's go."

Although it was getting light, they pulled up to her garage door with lights on, and saw nothing amiss. Tyler got out and looked at the lock set. As Lori approached, Tyler told her it looked like it had been jimmied.

Inside the garage, he went to the shelves where they had stowed the hi-fi amp. "Somebody grabbed the amp, unwrapped it, saw that it wasn't the rock unit, and wrapped it back up." Tyler looked around. "Nothing else bothered, no entry into the house?"

"Nothing. Barry?" she finally asked.

Tyler nodded. "Barry. And instead of me jumping on him, he'll probably stomp on me for tricking him!"

At the airport, Tyler's second look at the rock box was more interesting, as he had brought his set of spline wrenches.

The first panel removed showed a printed circuit board that Tyler recognized as a high-voltage power supply, and possibly more circuitry.

"Pretty hefty power supply, I think," he mumbled.

Other panels revealed hoses and wires running to other modules, one of which was a small motor, another to a battery pack. Further incursion showed a gear mechanism that seemed to be linked to rails that the meteorite rested on. The last screws removed the cylinder. Tyler inverted it and looked inside. The top of the cylinder was a dome, and when on the device, was directly above the edge of the rock where some type of roller apparently ran up and down the face of the meteorite.

Lori could see that Tyler was in his element. His face showed an intensity of thought that she had seen in no other person. She was in doubt that he would hear her, so she kept quiet, watched and listened.

Tyler talked slow and explanatory as though teaching a class. His forehead was shiny with sweat, a testament to his thinking process. He began as though the bell had rung to start class.

"The roller is abrasive, so it must be used to grind off tiny groups of atoms, meaning billions, of course. Anyway, these atoms fly up and get trapped in the dome, causing a tremendous upward force, easily lifting a two hundred pound man." He moved the box and peered from a different angle. "This power supply produces a very high voltage, enough to collect the trapped electrons." He scratched his head before continuing. "What happens to the nuclei?" he asked to no one in particular. Lori looked around as though to find an audience and realized they were alone. She sat quietly.

"The nuclei are going to build up one hell of a charge --." He broke off and shook his head.

Tyler turned the box at all angles to afford him the best view in every access panel. Each time he grunted, a sound that Lori had determined to be a failure comment.

On the side opposite the knob, Tyler found a small panel with no spline screws. He tried prying it off with a small screwdriver and at the second attempt the panel popped off and rattled on the floor.

Tyler looked inside the opening. "A connection, it looks like. Small, maybe quarter inch, inside, maybe outside threads. Huh." His last remark seemed to punctuate an end to his current investigation. He looked satisfyingly at Lori. "I don't know what he does with the nuclei, but the damn box is the work of a genius, I'll give him that."

With Lori's help, Tyler replaced all the panels and tightened down the spline-head screws. When they finished, he picked the box up and started for the door.

"Where to?" Lori asked him.

"C'mon, I'll show you."

The Sun had cleared the treetops to the east and poured its rays across the dashboard and directly into the eyes of the two occupants. Soon Tyler turned south and drove a few miles until coming to a small building near the banks of a stream. "Shaver's Fork Pumping Station," Tyler told Lori, seeing her quizzical expression.

Lori stayed in the car while Tyler went inside. A moment later, they were headed back the way they had come. "I don't think we were followed, so the box is safe for the moment.

Let's head for some breakfast." Then, he added, "I'll have a
little chat with Barry."

-16-

By the end of April, Tyler's and Lori's lives had returned to normal. Tyler had confronted Barry about breaking into Lori's garage and after he had confessed to the entry the two had agreed that Barry would replace the lockset, and would apologize to Lori. His obsession with the rock ended abruptly when his wife found out about his excursion to Lori's house and breaking in her garage. She scolded him as a mother would scold her child for breaking the cookie jar. Barry thought no more about stealing the rock after that, but still held Tyler to his word that the device would be destroyed, which helped him abandon his obsession.

Nothing was heard of Rossiter. No phone calls, no notes shoved under his door, nothing to indicate any interest in either Tyler or the rock. This worried Bridges in the beginning, but as time passed, thoughts of the man and his invention faded as April showers passed and summer got underway.

Lori, when not flying with Tyler on his charters, was busy with photographers, other artists and even engineers interested in the landscape as seen from the air. Usually they were short flights, which allowed her to end her workday early.

After a quick excursion on Wednesday, then watching her passenger deplane, Lori taxied to her hangar, and was surprised to find a man standing near the hanger door. She began the process of putting the Cessna indoors for the night when he approached.

"Good afternoon," he greeted, coming toward her. "Are you Miss Dennison?"

Lori nodded. The man approaching was short and stocky, broad-faced, with puffy jowls and a short neck. He stuck out a chunky hand and she felt his fingers tighten. "What can I do for you, Mister? --"

"Stewart, Galin Stewart. I need a quick flight to Lewis County airport." His voice was soft, but with an edge to it. "I just got in and the people at the terminal recommended you."

"Will I need to wait?" Lori asked, her eyes scrutinizing him.

"No, just drop me off, and you can be on your way," he answered, a quick smile brushing his lips. Lori agreed after making sure he understood that the airport had no facilities and unless someone was there to meet him, he would be unable to get transportation or food.

Stewart listened to her cautionary words, then smiled knowingly. "Don't worry about me," he said with confidence.

At her office the pricing was worked out. Stewart paid cash and waited while Lori filled out a flight plan. "Is all this necessary?" the young man asked. "I mean, it's just a short hop, I understand, to a tiny airstrip."

"Has to be done," Lori replied, writing. "Regulations, you know."

"Of course. I wasn't thinking – tell you what. I'll drop the flight plan off at flight service while you're getting the airplane ready. Save us some time. I really must get there right away."

Lori hesitated momentarily then acquiesced and handed Stewart the paper. He left and walked hurriedly away and Lori checked the plane. Her passenger returned and joined her in the cockpit. He fastened his seat belt and noticed the pilot staring at him. "Anything wrong?"

Lori blinked, then looked away. "It's just that – you look familiar. I think I've seen you before somewhere."

"Well, I've been somewhere before," he answered dryly.

After takeoff, Lori performed the required climbing left turn and set her course west by northwest. Stewart seemed unaffected by the bumpy ride. Lori had mentioned before they took off that the ride would be rough and that he might experience some severe altitude drops. Her passenger had shrugged nonchalantly and unconcerned as though she had informed him that there would be clouds in the sky.

Stewart's eyes were fixed across the nose of the airplane toward Route 33, which they were following. Lori noticed that rather than looking around, which most people do; her passenger seemed interested only in what was directly ahead. Stewart pointed along their line of flight. "What's that up ahead?"

Lori raised up slightly. "You mean the town?"

"Yes."

"That's Buckhannon."

"What are those buildings?"

"That's the campus of West Virginia Wesleyan College."

"Good. When we get there, please turn the plane to a heading of two-hundred and thirty degrees."

Lori frowned at her passenger. "What?"

"You heard me, Miss Dennison. Now . . . do it!"

Lori drew her brows together and her eyes began roving, trying to understand what was happening. She saw Stewart reaching into his pocket.

"If you don't do what I say, I'll slice your face up so the Hunchback of Notre Dame wouldn't give you a second look!"

Her hands shook as she began turning until the compass settled on the prescribed course. Lori, still shaking from her passenger's threat, reached into a map pocket on her left.

"You won't need a map. We're going to Braxton County Airport. And don't try anything funny. I know the landmarks . . . and I can fly this plane," he added. "Understand?"

The pilot shook her head yes.

Stewart was watching out the side, apparently verifying some landmarks. Lori, stiff with fear, glanced mechanically at the instruments. "Mind telling me what this is all about. I have no money --"

"All I can tell you is that someone wants to talk to you."

"Who?"

"Now, Miss Dennison, let's not make this any harder than necessary. My job is to bring you here. That's all."

Lori's mind was soon diverted from her hostage predicament as she fought the wind currents to keep the plane straight and level. Downdrafts would suck them down, making it necessary to add power and nose the airplane up. Updrafts threw them dangerously close to the 5000-foot level, the possible path of other aircraft. Fatigued, Lori fought the controls diligently for twenty minutes, and although not sure of the future, was almost happy to begin her descent to land.

Stewart watched carefully as the plane glided downward. His eyes tracked Interstate 79 on his right, then turned his attention to the front and watched idly as Lori lined up with the runway. He even seemed pleased as they landed, and gave an admiring look at the pilot. "Nice job, Miss Dennison. You are quite a pilot. If you do as you're told, nothing will happen to you."

Lori taxied the plane as instructed and killed the engine. As the propeller snapped to a stop, Stewart gestured for her to stay put, and climbed out. Lori sat stiff and tense, her head swiveling as though on a pivot, looking all around. In a moment she watched nervously as Stewart and another man approached.

Obeying a gesture for her to get out, Lori jumped off the protruding step and stood down. Stewart spoke quietly.

"Please do not try anything, or you will be sedated. Do you understand?"

Lori shook her head slowly.

"Good. Just walk with us to a car over there and get in the back seat. I will be in the front, my partner, here, will drive."

Lori ducked and climbed into a large limousine. Stewart and the other man watched, then followed suit. Once inside, Stewart turned toward Lori. "We're going to Rossiter Dynamics. I think you know the way," he said with sarcasm.

Lori took a quick breath. "Now I know where I saw you. You were at Gerald Frank's memorial service, weren't you?"

Stewart glanced at the driver. "I would advise you forget you ever saw me . . . now or then."

When she last traversed the road, it was late at night, and she retained very little details of the trip. When the limo entered the parking lot, Lori sat upright, surprised. Unlike her previous visit when the lot was empty, the weekday afternoon version was exactly opposite. Cars were parked everywhere. They were in rows, along pathways, hugging the narrow access roads, even pulled over on the grassy lawn. The upstairs manufacturing plant was in full production.

The limo followed a narrow strip of asphalt that skirted the end of the building and curved around to a small parking area containing only one car. Lori's nervousness increased markedly as she recognized the lone doorway, which she knew, led to the basement area. Images flashed through her mind as she recalled pulling the heavy metal door open and sneaking inside and finding the guard holding Tyler and Barry at gunpoint. She shuddered as she remembered striking the man on the head.

Lori's expectations of seeing more people were diminished quickly as she was led inside. The giant room was dim as only a single bank of lights was on. She was led around the deserted workstations, to a door in the far side. Stewart opened it and snapped on a light.

Lori stepped in cautiously, not believing her eyes. Had she not known better, she would have sworn they had taken her to a luxurious hotel. The room was bright and cheerful, lavishly furnished with a couch, two easy chairs, a coffee table and a large desk. She could see a small room with a bed on the left, and a galley directly ahead. To the right was the bathroom. Stewart stood in the doorway. "I trust you will be comfortable here, Miss Dennison. The kitchen is fully stocked and there are some clothes in the closet and drawers. You may watch TV, and there is reading material in the bookcase."

He quickly stepped back and closed the door. Lori heard a click and her pulse raced. She instinctively rushed to the door and twisted the lock, then pounded. Realizing the futility of this, she sat down and looked around, tears welling in her eyes. Her thoughts turned to Tyler.

Tyler finished his work for the day and drove directly to the airport, whistling. Their plans for the evening included dinner at an upscale restaurant, some dancing at a local lounge afterward, then home to do their own lounging in his loft. Lori's schedule showed one quick charter, which, she estimated would put her back at the airport by 3 P.M.

Finding her hangar door open, Tyler assumed that for some reason her return had been delayed. He looked at his watch. It was after 5 P.M., and a troubled look crossed his face as he strolled into flight service.

The attendant there showed him her flight plan. It showed a trip to Weston with no wait and a straight return. She was almost an hour overdue. Tyler left a note on her desk and drove home. At his driveway, he once again had a feeling of abandonment. He scratched his head and went inside.

-17-

Tyler returned to the airport around 6 P.M. and went directly to flight services. When asked, he was told that there was no way of knowing whether or not Lori had landed at Weston. The attendant told Tyler that he had checked with nearby airfields and that none had reported seeing Lori's airplane. Worried now, Tyler thanked him and left.

Hoping for a call, he stayed around his cabin all evening, cleaning up the mess made by whoever had ransacked the place earlier. He paced the floor, tried to immerse himself in a book or magazine, which he impatiently tossed aside. He made numerous trips to the kitchen but with no appetite surfacing he found himself back near the telephone.

At 7:30, it rang.

Nearly falling to reach it, he panted a hello.

"Mister Bridges?"

"Yes," Tyler's voice, fraught with anticipation, cracked.

"First, please understand that Miss Dennison is safe."

"May I speak --"

"I'm sorry, but you must take my word for it. She is well, and will not be harmed if you listen and do exactly as you're told. Otherwise, I cannot guarantee her safety."

"Look, you." Tyler growled, his muscles tensing. "If you harm her, I will --"

"I told you," the voice interrupted, "she is safe. Please wait."

Tyler took a gulp of air to speak, then realized there was no one on the line. His heart was racing, his jaws bulged as he clenched his teeth in anger. His head was beginning to pound.

Another voice that he didn't recognize came on the line. "Mister Bridges. Please bring the stolen device back to Rossiter Dynamics Laboratory this Friday night."

"What about Miss Dennison? I demand to talk to her!"

"Your demands are inconsequential. If you follow the instructions carefully and surrender the box, we will turn her over to you unharmed and no worse for wear."

Tyler sounded deflated. "Go ahead. What am I to do?"

Instructions were repeated; he was to bring the box on Friday night at midnight to Rossiter Dynamics, and he was to come to the rear door where someone would meet him. He would then surrender the box, and Lori would be returned to him at that time.

"When that has been done, you will be free to leave," the voice said.

Tyler said he agreed, hoping his voice did not divulge his real feelings, which were that he had no intention of doing as ordered for the simple fact that he knew his life, as well as Lori's, would be worth nothing when he surrendered the box. His mind wandered back to Gerald's memorial, and how he had the strange feeling that Rossiter, or someone paid by him, had done Gerald in.

For the next hour after he hung up, he sat, slumped in his chair, legs over the arm, scratching his head. That Lori was safe at the moment, and he felt sure she was, made his thought process function without restriction. One hour later he unfurled his long legs, got up and called Barry. After he answered and they greeted, Barry sensed the tightness in his friend's voice. He asked Tyler what was wrong.

"They've got Lori, Bear."

After listening to a cornucopia of Barry's profanities, Tyler continued. "All good and well. They want to do a switch Friday night and I need your help."

"What time do you want me at your place?"

After he told him and hung up, Tyler drove to Shaver's Fork, retrieved the device, and returned home. On his workbench in the shed, Tyler again removed the panels that exposed the rock, the circuitry, and the wiring and plumbing. Again he looked for and was unable to locate any clue as to how Rossiter disposed of the small nuclei after their electrons had been shaken loose. This would leave a heavy unbalanced particle called an ion that, if not supplanted by enough electrons, would soon build up quite a charge. At the least, it would deliver a paralyzing shock to anyone in contact with it. In a worst case scenario, if the box did actually work, it would probably explode after only a minute, maybe even seconds. Tyler chuckled, thinking how that would please Barry.

The small opening with the connector puzzled him. He carefully looked for another panel that up to now had been missed by either him or Lori, but could find no more. The connector obviously was for some remote control unit.

Thursday allowed more time for Tyler to chew over the problem of how to make the box operate. Whenever he was not thinking about his job, his mind automatically resumed with the box's analysis.

Friday evening Barry came, jumped out of his truck and bear-hugged Tyler. "Let's go get these bastards so I can tromp that piece of shit into oblivion!" the big man roared.

Tyler managed to calm him down long enough to get him into the house where they could talk and plan. As they downed coffee Tyler gave him the details of the kidnapping and the consequent exchange agreement, and some of his own thoughts. "I'm damn sure not going to go to the door, hand them the box, and wait for them to produce Lori."

Barry listened intently, as though waiting for the next shoe to drop. Then as the remainder of the plot was completed, he sat back and grinned. "Sounds like a plan to me," he admitted happily.

Trying to kill time by talking about their fishing excursions didn't work, as both men became more anxious as the evening wore on. Tyler became dubious about Barry's mental state, concerned that he might become violent and risk Lori's life or at least her well being. At the moment, the big guy was displaying signs of hating those that had kidnapped her, and was contemplating what he might do to them when they met.

Tyler looked at his watch at 10:30 and nodded to Barry. The two grabbed their jackets and headed for Tyler's car.

By midnight they again entered the parking lot at Rossiter Dynamics, found it empty as before, and drove around the back. Tyler headed for the most distant point in view of the rear door and backed his vehicle into it. They sat quietly for they had a few minutes before Tyler was expected.

Inside, Lori was pacing, trying to keep calm, but was feeling increasingly claustrophobic. Her captive quarters had been adequate, and she was neither hungry nor sleepy, but her desire to return to freedom was engulfing her. She could think of nothing else, and yearned for someone to talk to. She watched the clock on the wall as though it was a time lock, and would click open the door at any time.

Footsteps approached, and her hand went to her heart as to quell the rapid beating. The door clicked and opened. The stocky man who had brought her here swept his hand to escort her out. "If your boyfriend has done his part, you will be free in a moment."

Lori's first reaction was to thank him, but an instant later she realized how stupid that was, and her thoughts returned to Tyler. She again meandered around the tables and benches, following the short man through the large room and heading for the door, her excitement growing with each step.

The steel door was closed, and her captor put his finger to his lips for quiet. He stood, sleepy-eyed, and shifted his weight as they waited. Lori wanted to move, to run, to yell, but kept silent and still. She watched the door handle, waiting for it to turn and let her out.

Suddenly there was a thump at the door.

Outside, Tyler knocked hard three times, then stood back.

The man known as Stewart opened the door, saw a man he believed to be Tyler Bridges, and noticed that he was empty-handed.

Lori couldn't control herself, and yelled, "Tyler!"

"Wait!" Stewart told her, his hand suddenly filled with a revolver.

Tyler held both hands high to indicate no aggression. He strained to see around the stocky-built man. "Lori? Are you all right?"

Lori nodded yes, then tried to move forward only to be stopped by Stewart. "What's going on? Where's the box, Bridges?"

Tyler pointed backward. "I suggest you look over my shoulders, Mister."

Both Stewart and Lori looked.

Barry Southerland stood with the meteorite box held high above his head. Once Tyler was sure Stewart had seen Barry, be lowered his hands. "That is a friend of mine, Mister. You let Miss Dennison loose now. Lori, you walk straight toward Barry. If anyone interferes, that man will throw the device down, smashing it to bits. Understand? When Lori is safely in the car, he will place the machine down on the blacktop and leave." Finished, he stepped to the side and began backing away from the doorway, gesturing that Lori was to follow him.

Suddenly a wry smile crossed Stewart's lips. He stopped the girl as she started through and tossed a nod to Tyler. "Now, I suggest you look behind you."

Tyler glanced around. Barry was not to be seen and a man was coming toward them with the box under his arm. He dropped a long round club he was carrying.

"Barry!" Lori cried, and tried to run out and was held by Stewart. "Leave him," Stewart shouted, "we have our orders." He pushed Lori backward until another man grabbed her.

Lori and Tyler were herded through the spacious room toward the suite in which Lori was held captive. They were shoved in the room and the door locked.

Stewart and the man with the box crossed the room and entered the door leading to a workshop. The assistant placed the box on a table as instructed. "Now what?"

Stewart gave him a disgusted look. "We stay here and await orders. You hit that guy out there hard?"

The other man nodded. "He's probably dead," he replied, a malicious smile crossing his lips. "I smacked him good."

"Good. Now sit down somewhere and shut up."

In the suite, Lori was sobbing in Tyler's arms, too upset to talk. Tyler stroked her head until her trembling stopped. "It's OK, Lori," he soothed. "We're going to get out of this. Don't worry."

She finally composed herself enough to talk. "What about Barry?" she managed to ask.

Tyler forced himself to look confident. "Barry's tougher than iron." He gave Lori a wide smile. "He's probably trying to break into this place right now. Please don't worry. Now let me look around."

Tyler walked into the small bedroom, returned, and went to the kitchen. Lori heard some rattling sounds, drawers opening, closing, then Tyler returned and walked to the door and listened. "I think they're still out there. I can hear someone talking."

Lori noticed that Tyler's head was angled and slightly inclined, the sign of his deep thinking process. She watched as he walked absent-mindedly to a chair and sat down. Realizing that communicating with him would be difficult now, she went to the kitchen and put on a pot of coffee. When she returned, he looked at her. "Coffee?"

"I thought we might just make the best of the situation. Besides, I figured you might need something to keep you awake."

"Thanks. I already have that."

"Meaning?"

"Every time I close my eyes, I see hundreds of dark-skinned, towel-headed men standing on little platforms, gradually rising to drop bombs down chimneys, smokestacks, power plants, schools, even the White House. It's like some kind of cheap movie about aliens."

Lori suddenly realized the vision of this man, how he could almost predict the future, determine what was going to happen, just by those obsessive moments of his.

"And something else is driving me crazy."

"Me?" Lori asked as she sat beside him.

"You? Oh, hell no. You're the only thing that stands between me and the looney bin."

Lori's hand went to her heart. "Oh, Ty, you say the nicest things," she jested.

"The code," he said in a serious tone.

"What about it? I thought we, you broke it."

Tyler scratched his head. "Near the end of the paper there were a few smudged letters I couldn't figure out," he admitted, "and it's driving me crazy."

"What letters?"

"DG DBX \PT. And there was a space between the G and the D, which I think means the D is a 4. And the letter after X is smudged, but I think it is an A."

"Then, that would make it DG4BXAPT, right?" Lori asked.

Tyler grimaced. "Yes. Now, *you* can start obsessing over it."

Sipping coffee, they sat at length in silence, both within their own thoughts. Lori kept writing invisible numbers on her palm and looked at them, frowning. Tyler looked at her and chuckled. "Keep that up, and you'll be as nuts as I am."

Lori stared at her hand. Her facial expressions changed as ideas ran through her mind and were rejected. Suddenly her eyes widened and an unbelievable look came across her face.

"Ty! Ty, I've got it!" she said excitedly.

Tyler looked up, startled. "Got what?"

"The code, silly. I know what it means!"

Tyler raised his eyebrows, waiting.

"It means Drawings 4 Box is in apartment. The drawings are in here!"

Tyler kissed her. "Honey, you're a genius. All we have to do now is find it. C'mon." He grabbed her hand. "Pick a room."

First Tyler searched the desk and found nothing. Lori disappeared into the bedroom.

She emptied drawers and examined their bottoms. They both looked in all the kitchen cabinets then searched the laundry area. Lori stood by the couch and looked around. Tyler came out of the bathroom holding a quart jar. "Stuck with putty to the bottom of the commode tank," he announced. His expression resembled the cat that ate the canary.

A tap on the door brought the two captives to their feet. Lori's hand went to her heart, Tyler's mouth flew open and he stuffed the bottle under the couch cushion.

"You guys in there?" a voice said.

Tyler pounded on the door. "Barry? We're here."

"Hold on. I'll get you out! Stand back!"

-18-

Unlike a normal door opening, the one to the suite suddenly began cracking, broke away from the frame, and fell headlong on the floor at the feet of Tyler and Lori, erupting a dust cloud that made them both cough.

Barry's appearance in the doorway was shocking and resembled something from a scary movie. Blood was crusted from above his ear to his shoulder. His face and beard were grimy, with traces of tar and asphalt streaking from his forehead to his chin. His clothes were torn and dirty, his hands cut and bruised. He threw aside a concrete barrier he had confiscated from the parking lot, and staggered forward.

Lori, tears streaming, hugged the big man as Tyler grabbed his hand to steady him. Finally Lori stood back. "I'll get some stuff from the bathroom."

Looking exhausted, he stumbled to a chair. Lori returned with bottles, cloths, and a pan of water. As she carefully dabbed, wiped and cleaned, the big man sat, his eyes vacant, an occasional flinch as Lori's work caused a pain. Finally he looked at Tyler.

"I was at the car, and everything went black. When I woke up I was lying across the marshes in a stand of trees. I must have dragged myself there, but I don't remember. After a few minutes I happened to see a short, stocky man leave and go around the corner. So I figured there was probably one man inside guarding you."

"Take it easy, Barry," Lori cautioned as she continued cleaning the wounds.

"Anyway, when I could stand without everything getting fuzzy, I crossed the parking lot and went to the door." He stopped, remembering. "First, I went back and picked up the club that I had been hit with."

The big man continued to tell them that he remembered the code and opened the door. The room was dimly lit, the only light coming from a nearby doorway.

"I saw a guy dozing behind a table, so I sneaked up on him. He woke just as I reached him, and he tried to pull a gun. I swatted that sonofabitch good." Barry chuckled. "He ended up on the floor about ten feet away. So I took his gun, trussed him up like a steer at branding, knocked on a few doors, and here I am."

Tyler put a hand on Barry's shoulder. "I'm sure as hell glad you're on our side. You feel like traveling?"

Barry, resembling a mummy, smiled. "I would very much like to get out of this place."

"I've got to find that box, then we can leave."

Tyler sent Barry to the forward rooms and he and Lori searched the rooms off to the side. Lori saw the man unconscious on the floor and veered around him, shivering.

Their first doorway led them into a room full of tools, machines, and supplies that would make any engineer or hobbyist envious. Metal-cutting tools abounded. Lathes, saws, drills, and grinders, all finely tuned and ready for precision work. Tyler looked closely at a tile-cutting saw that no doubt was used to cut stone. After studying it a minute, he looked directly above and smiled. The ceiling was discolored and there was evidence of the roof leaking on the saw table. This was, he theorized, the saw used to cut the stone for fitting into the rack in the box.

Lori tugged at him as a mother would tug her child away from a toy exhibit. "Sorry," he apologized.

The next room they entered was nearly empty and warranted only a cursory search.

Barry joined Lori and Tyler as they entered the last room. There, on the table just as it was earlier, stood the box, it's dull finish shining in the door light. Tyler, not trusting Barry yet, swept it up. "Let's go," he whispered.

Barry opened the outside door and stepped out to look around. Seeing nothing, he waved to Tyler and Lori. They stepped out into cold, damp air, Lori hugging the jar of papers to her. Tyler saw how light it was and checked his watch. It read 7:20. "We need to get out of here now," he urged them.

With Tyler and the box in front and Lori with her jar of diagrams in the back, Barry drove off. He drove slowly along the narrow access beside the building, and when they cleared the corner a car was just coming into the lot. It was big and black, with 2 people inside. Barry tromped the accelerator.

On a direct collision course, Barry hunched over the wheel. "They want to play chicken, do they?" he hissed. "Well, I'll play!"

Both Tyler and Lori yelled Barry's name, then saw that the other car had swerved to miss them. The vehicle's driver was swerving, trying to gain control of the car. Barry laughed, an insane gurgling that shocked everyone. "That'll teach 'em," he said loudly, looking back.

Lori watched behind them as Tyler's car careened the tiny curves, wheels screeching, toward the airport road. "Nothing, yet," she reported.

"Barry? Drop us off at the airport then head for my house, get your truck and go home. You'll be OK then. Lori and I will fly somewhere safe for now."

"Did I hear a shot back there?" Barry asked.

"Maybe they had a flat tire," Lori said, looking around. "They aren't in sight yet."

Before the car had completely stopped, doors opened and the two got out, waved goodbye and headed for Lori's airplane.

"Watch for them," Lori told Tyler as she tested the controls and twisted the starter.

The plane came to life and began vibrating as the engine settled into an idle. Lori pushed the throttle forward and they taxied to the active runway and lined up. As the wheels left the ground, Tyler watched the road from Rossiter Dynamics. "Nothing yet. That's strange."

"I'll take it," Lori answered. "Now, where to?"

"Any airport with a restaurant and a bathroom."

"That'll be CKB, uh, Clarksburg. They have a full terminal there."

In thirty minutes they landed on Runway 3 at Clarksburg and were guided to a parking place just outside the terminal.

Tyler had the jar containing the roll of diagrams and found a quiet corner in the restaurant and unrolled them. As he spread them out, Lori returned from the restroom.

Whether it was the restaurant's quiet clanking of dishes, the dim lighting, or the fact that they were away from danger, Lori appeared serene. They ordered breakfast and while waiting, Tyler studied the first drawing.

It was hand-drawn, quite unprofessional when compared to the precision construction of the box itself. It was a side view and top view of the box. Lori brought her chair next to his and watched, apparently excited.

The side view showed a rough sketch of the meteorite, trimmed flat on one end. It lay on a rack of some kind, which allowed it to move horizontally. "See that little roller that runs up and down the face? It gradually wears away the rock, so the rock needs to be fed into the roller."

Lori, hands cupping her chin, nodded.

Directly over the roller and atop the cylinder was an upside-down cone, a collector of some sort, Tyler figured. There were wires running to a module, which Tyler had already assessed as a high-voltage power supply. "This collects the electrons after they lose energy," he whispered. "This is a pretty crude diagram, but maybe there's more." He turned it behind, exposing the next page, which was mostly notes, apparently based on initial tests. Tyler's eyes widened. "This is Gerald's writing," he exclaimed. The two of them began reading.

> *The empty atom is in existence less than a second.*
>
> *Need to sweep the rock at least 3 times per second to test. Roller sweep rate must be increased as more life is needed.*

> *Need to work on gas nozzles for directional control.*
>
> *Gas prevents buildup of positive ions*

Tyler put the papers down. "What kind of gas?" he asked rhetorically.

The remaining pages were full of weight and load data, correlating the speed of the roller to lift strength. There were notes on deterioration of the cone and estimates on lift versus rock volume. The calculations showed that the stone in the box would sustain lift for 67 hours. That meant Rossiter could slice the stone into dozens of small chunks that would be large enough to provide the necessary lift to sabotage a power plant. Reading this data, Tyler shook his head in amazement.

There was no information on the metal used in the cone, nor was there any information about the outside connection via the small connector.

"Well," Tyler said, shoving the papers aside. "That's why there were so many gas tanks standing around."

"Scary, that's what it is," Lori quipped. "Maybe Barry is right. We need to destroy it."

Tyler looked at her and raised his eyebrows in agreement.

They had a leisure breakfast of eggs, bacon and toast, and managed to sip 2 cups of coffee before Tyler cleared his throat.

"I don't want to fly back yet, as that is what we would be expected to do. I want them to play our game."

"Ty?"

"What?"

"You're not wanting to hang on to this thing so you can experiment with it, are you?" Lori's eyes were probing, scanning his face.

"I must admit that I considered it," he admitted, "but then I would have to kill Barry, wouldn't I?" he added, then laughed.

"Where to now?" Lori asked.

"Back to your hangar," he answered. "I'll remove the rock, then we'll call Barry so he can come and destroy the box. Once Rossiter knows we don't have the thing any more, and that I have destroyed the paperwork, maybe he'll go away."

On the flight back, Tyler continued to show an interest in the drawings, looking for what he didn't know. His curiosity was centered around the nagging problem of how the ion level was kept low. Finally he stuffed the papers in his jacket pocket, and sat back, engulfed in brooding.

Lori was, as usual, caught up in the flight, not just the technical aspects, but also the beauty of the sky, the clouds, and the land slipping by below. Mentally she identified the rivers, lakes, churches, courthouses, and railroads as they passed beneath, for this was the navigation of the true pilot. Lindbergh, Earhart, the mail pilots and a thousand others found their way all over the world by these methods, and Lori practiced them constantly. When the radios failed, proficiency in this method would determine life or death.

Since the day was clear, her altitude of 5500 feet provided her a good view of the vast Monongahela Forest. She had flown easterly, then turned south, and began letting down as soon as she spotted the highway that ran north of the airfield.

Tyler came out of his slump as she taxied to the hangar, anxious to examine the box again. Thoughts of selling the amber rock soon crowded out his ambitions to make the box fly.

"I want to call Barry, see if he made it home OK. Maybe we can get together with them soon." Lori offered.

"Fine," Tyler said as he carried the box inside.

Lori grabbed the phone in her office and punched the numbers. "Hi, Robin, this is Lori." She frowned. "What?"

Tyler glanced up as Lori cradled the receiver. "Barry's not there. Robin says some man called and said Barry wouldn't be home for a long time."

"So?"

"So, Barry's been kidnapped!"

Tyler looked at her incredulously. "Good God. Does Rossiter do anything but kidnap people?"

Lori smiled sadly. "Well, if he came up here and shot you and me and took the stone, there would be a full scale investigation, wouldn't there? So, this way, no one can talk, and we end up in his own back yard, where he can eliminate you, us, and nobody the wiser."

-19-

Tyler continued to look at Lori.

"Robin said she received a message a little while ago saying that her husband had been taken and she was to contact you with a phone number to call."

"Jesus," Tyler blurted out angrily. "How did they get him so fast?"

"I'll bet they've got an airplane," she said, then started out. "You call this number. I'm going to flight service. Back in a few."

Tyler drew a weary breath and called the number.

"Rossiter speaking."

"Rossiter, this is Bridges."

"Yes, Bridges. You are causing me a great deal of trouble. I had planned on releasing you and your friends, but when you stole my invention – and the papers – well, I just have to get them back. I have commitments --"

"What about Barry. Is he all right?"

"Of course."

"So I assume you want me to bring you the box."

"Very perceptive of you, Mister Bridges. You have two hours to produce the device and the paperwork at my laboratory – you know where that it, I take it? Anyway, those are the terms. Otherwise I shall tell Missus Southerland that you have killed her husband. Do you understand?"

"I understand."

"Good. Two hours." Click.

When Lori returned, Tyler was pacing back and forth.

"A Mooney landed here a little while ago, and somebody rented a car. What's wrong, Ty?"

Tyler told her the deadline. "It's two-o'clock now, so we have until four."

"Then let's get going. I'll need to gas up first – where are you going?"

"Just to get my rock."

The return trip to Braxton airport was solemn, with neither party feeling much like conversation. Lori on occasion glanced toward her passenger but said nothing. Tyler watched the landscape slide beneath him. Neither had the usual fascination of flying together, just a dreaded interest in the destination.

Finally Lori broke the silence. "What happens when we get to the airport?"

Tyler grimaced as though stretching the stiffness from his face. "I really don't know, Lori. I guess I'll rent a car and try to get Barry free before I turn the device and plans over to him." He lay against the headrest. Lori looked hard at him. "You mean you're giving up?"

"No, but --"

"But, hell, Tyler. We've got some flying time yet, so you come up with a plan." She was shouting, both in anger and to rise above the engine noise.

Tyler held his hands in surrender position. "OK. Don't worry, I'll think of something," he said. "Now leave me alone."

Silence again fell in the cockpit, the drone of the engine changing as Lori began her approach to Braxton. Tyler's last instruction to her was to park her plane in a position to leave quickly. "You're going to stay in the plane this time, Lori."

"No!"

"Yes, you are. Do you want to see Barry again?" He watched Lori nod shamefully. "Then you stay with the plane. I'll get him free, but we're going to need a quick departure from you. Besides, having you along will only increase chances of him getting more leverage on me through you. You understand that, don't you?"

Lori mimicked Tyler by slumping in the seat and producing a pouty lower lip. "I understand," she said in a reluctant tone.

By the time Tyler had rented a car, Lori had taxied to the fence and was in the process of swinging the tail around to point the nose directly toward the runway. He took the box and the paper roll and stowed it in the rental. Lori met him under the wing, raised on her toes, and kissed him. "You come back soon, hear?"

Tyler looked into her eyes and nodded slowly. He cleared his throat. "I will," he said, turning away.

When he arrived at the plant, he experienced deja vu, like some returning nightmare. He drove around the back of the building, and checked his watch. It was 3:45. Tyler climbed out, and with his ransom under his arm, headed for the door. He punched in the security code and opened the door as though he was coming home. He raised the box with one hand above his head.

"So that's how you got in," a voice said.

Kyle Rossiter stood to the side, a revolver dangling from his hand. "Who gave you the code?" he asked.

"Gerald managed to slip me a message before you killed him," Tyler admitted.

Rossiter's face showed no change. "But I didn't kill Gerald Franks. Whatever gave you that idea?"

Tyler shrugged indifference. "Just figured you did, that's all. Or paid someone to do it."

"I don't kill people just for fun," Rossiter stated. "Gerald was no threat to me. I had information connecting him to an embezzlement scheme, and if anything would've gone wrong, I would have turned him in to the authorities."

Rossiter backed up and stopped. Tyler saw that he was beside Barry. The older man placed the gun at Barry's head.

"So, Mister Bridges. Please put the box down carefully on that table, then lay the papers beside them."

Tyler shook his head slowly. "You are an intelligent man, Rossiter, and you should realize that doing that would put me in a very vulnerable position. You also know that if I fall, the box drops. I also removed the top panels."

Rossiter's eyes turned hard, and he looked askew toward Tyler. "The Mexican standoff thing doesn't work on me, Bridges. Either put the box down or I shoot your friend. Then I will shoot you. You have exactly five seconds."

Tyler suddenly realized that his plans no longer held any threat.

"One."

The gun pressed against Barry's temple. Tyler looked at his friend.

"Two."

Tyler glanced around in a futile attempt to find something with which to stop this process.

"Three."

Barry's face was shiny with sweat. Tyler's arms were getting numb and he heard the unmistakable sound of a pistol cocking.

"Four!"

"OK!" Tyler shouted quickly. Watching Rossiter, he lowered the box, stepped over and slowly placed it on a nearby table.

Rossiter pulled away and kept the weapon trained on Southerland. "All right, gentlemen, please move slowly toward that door." He nodded to a doorway that Tyler knew to be a small, empty room with no windows. It was obvious that the plan was to keep them there until cover of darkness, at which time they would be taken out and murdered.

As the two men reluctantly moved toward the doorway, Tyler caught a glimpse of movement near the outside doorway. An instant later the room was plunged into pitch darkness.

"Go, Barry!" Tyler shouted, and both men hit the floor and began crawling, bumping and slamming into furniture, trying to put distance between them and Rossiter's last known location. Tyler heard noises near the outside door.

Flickering, the lights came back on. The two kept low and scrambled farther away from Rossiter's gun. They froze, listened, and heard nothing. All they could see was table legs. Their view resembled looking under a corral of horse's legs. Tyler spotted Barry's foot and began moving toward him.

Rossiter had moved back to the worktable where Tyler had laid the device. He began attaching the rod and handle then quickly plugged the makeshift cable and hose into their sockets.

Nearby, on the floor, both men heard the clanking, which was followed by a hissing sound then a soft buzzing noise. Tyler frowned questioningly toward Barry then suddenly gestured for Barry to get down low.

Rossiter laughed as he began to rise. "Stand up where I can see you!" His voice was commanding, and strained. "Otherwise, I will shoot you on sight. Your call, gentlemen!"

Both men were lying flat, squirming beneath tables to remain out of sight. Bullets would penetrate the workbenches and they would be sitting targets if Rossiter spotted them.

Rossiter's platform began moving forward slowly as he began a search pattern, moving toward the rear wall, slowly, deliberately, his eyes scanning the floor much like a soaring hawk watches a field for mice.

On the hard floor, beneath frail protection, the two men froze at their positions, waiting and listening, hoping for some way to escape from the killer overhead. Tyler, sweat running in his eyes, scanned the floor for a safer spot.

Floating near the ceiling, Rossiter kept up his dialogue of threats and promises, intertwined with strains of humming. "Come on out, boys. You don't stand a chance!"

Suddenly he jerked his head and stared toward the center of the room. "Who the hell --"

A figure dressed in black, his face covered, yanked the supply cable. By the time Rossiter realized what was happening the man had run through the open door and disappeared outside.

Rossiter's platform suddenly lost levitation and dropped rapidly, striking a tabletop. Rossiter was propelled sideways onto the floor, striking his left shoulder, his head bouncing on his outstretched arm. He lay quietly.

Seeing this, Barry yelled, "Come on!" and made his way across the tables and grabbed the device. He yanked the cables and hose free and started for the door.

As he ran by and just before following Barry outside, Tyler glanced down and noticed that Rossiter was coming to, shaking his head slowly. He was gripping his pistol tightly. The two men ran through the open doorway, and Tyler slammed it shut.

Seconds later, they jumped in the car, and as they backed up, the door opened and Rossiter appeared and raised his weapon.

Tyler heard a shot from behind him then saw a puff of dust at the doorframe. Rossiter dove back in the building.

The two men looked at each other, shrugged, then careened around the corner, across the parking lot, and headed down the road to the airport, all the while Tyler was looking back and seeing no one.

"Who was that?" Tyler asked, his voice incredulous.

"Beats me. But whoever it was, I'm grateful."

Just short of being reckless, Barry screamed around the curves, stomping first the brakes then the accelerator, whipping the steering wheel much like a captain of a small boat during a storm on the seas, finally skidding to a stop in front of the rental agency.

"Remind me to never, ever ride with you again," said Tyler. "Drop these keys in that slot, then come to the plane. Lori's waiting."

Seeing them coming, she had started the engine. Tyler held the door against the prop wash as Barry climbed in. Once Tyler had closed the door, Lori throttled up the engine to taxi.

When the plane was lined up with the runway, Barry shouted, "Look!"

Tyler saw the car coming down the road, heading for the end of the runway. "Let's get out of here, Lori. He's got a weapon!"

Lori gunned the engine and the plane picked up speed rapidly. Rossiter's car turned off the road and crossed a short field of grass before it bounced upon the asphalt of the runway. He was directly in front of the plane and Lori's knuckles turned white on the wheel. Suddenly puffs of smoke popped up from the speeding car, and blotches appeared in the windscreen. "Get down!" Lori yelled, and pulled back on the yoke.

The airplane cleared his car by only a few feet. Rossiter slowed down, turned off the runway and bumped back on the road. He continued on to the airport hangars. There, he jumped out and pulled open the doors to his hangar.

With its short retractable landing gear and characteristically straight tail, the Mooney stood, gleaming in the center of the big hangar. Rossiter ran for the tow rod and snapped it into place. Sweating and grunting, he began pulling and steering the airplane out of the hangar. Once outside, he tossed the rod aside and climbed in. He scanned his instruments and swore. The fuel gauges read almost zero! He looked in the direction the Cessna had taken then called for a fuel truck.

-20-

As they continued climbing, Barry finished fastening his seat belt. He leaned forward. "Hey guys, I've got news!"

Lori leaned back. "What?"

"That guy Rossiter has a plane."

Tyler nodded a confirmation, looking at Lori.

"The Mooney," she affirmed.

"Let's change course, Lori," Tyler suggested, "maybe head for Parkersburg. Buy us more time, in case he does decide to chase us."

Tyler marveled at Lori's uncanny ability for determining course headings as he felt the plane bank and turn. Her experience of flying in West Virginia was obvious. Knowing how to fly was one thing, but knowing where you were at all times was the mark of a good pilot. And Lori was surely that. Never had he loved her or respected her more than at this minute.

Flying northwest over mostly forest and vegetation gave Tyler time to study the device again. He had removed the tall handle and cable and had stowed them on the floor.

Barry watched him with skeptical eyes as Tyler shifted the box around, looking at the various openings. He consulted the papers from time to time and tried to correlate something he read to the box on his lap. Suddenly conscious of Barry's gaze, he turned. "Don't worry, Barry. I'm going to remove the stone and then it's all yours. Can't do it now, though – no tools."

Satisfied, Barry sat back and began gazing lazily at the forests below. To him, roads crossed every which way, going left, right, or disappearing beneath the plane. To Lori, they were checkmarks used to track her course. Her eyes scanned the windows, looking for anything on a collision course, and then she would shift her attention to the ground and its myriad of markers, all of which served to confirm her plane's location in the sky. "Ty?"

"Yes?"

"The Mooney is twice as fast as this plane, you know."

"Thanks for the info," he said sarcastically, "maybe he won't be able to find us."

Tyler glanced back. Barry had his eyes closed and his breathing was slow and rhythmical. He leaned toward Lori. "You know when I told you about those bouts of loneliness and abandonment I felt a couple of times?"

Lori smiled. "The ones you didn't have when I was around?"

"Er, yes. Well, I just wanted you to know I don't have them any more," he answered in a tone of finality.

"That's wonderful, dearest, but what say you study your toy and let me fly this thing. We'll talk more about that stuff when there isn't an airplane engine roaring three feet from us."

"What's that over there?" Tyler asked.

"That's Interstate seventy-nine, and right back there," she pointed to her right, "is where Route thirty-three intersects it. We'll be at Parkersburg in about a half-hour, all things considered."

The flight was rough, but Barry slept even though his head was bobbing and bouncing.

The voice came across Lori's headphones clearly and distinctly. "Miss Dennison? Can you read me?"

Her eyes widened and she glanced around, a frightened look on her face. She indicated for Tyler to put on his phones.

"Miss Dennison? Can you read? Over."

Tyler frowned, also twisting, turning his head. "It's Rossiter. Might as well answer him."

Lori snapped a switch, which changed radios from her primary to the secondary, which she kept tuned to the emergency frequency. "Yes? What is it?"

Nothing for a moment, then, "Go to two. nine. point. zero."

Lori ratcheted the knobs that changed the channel to the new frequency. "Yes?"

Another pause, then: "I am directly beneath you. Climb to fifty-five, and turn to zero nine zero."

"Why? Where are you talking about?"

"Never mind," came the reply. "Just do as you're told and do not try to use your Com one radio. Understood?"

Lori acknowledged and began a climbing turn. When the plane reached the designated altitude and course, the radio crackled again. "Good. Now, fly this heading, do not communicate. Remember, I am directly below you, and I am armed!"

For the first time, Tyler saw Lori desperately trying to maintain her composure. Her eyes had a dismal look to them and her knuckles were constantly wringing the control wheel. Her shoulders were slumped, and she stared out the windshield through eyes that seemed visionless.

"Snap out of it, Lori!" Tyler yelled, then shook her. "We're not giving up yet!"

Lori's head jerked as she came out of her stupor. "Sorry, Ty, but I just --," her voice broke off.

"It's OK, honey. We're going to make it. Stay focused. We don't want to crash in that lake down there . . . it'll get us all wet." He grinned, hoping the gesture was infectious.

Lori glanced over and forced a smile.

Suddenly Tyler's eyes froze. "Wet? Water?" He straightened up. "Water! That's how he did it!"

Barry had woken up. "That's how who did what?"

"That's how Rossiter neutralized the ions!" Tyler's eyes took on a triumphant stare. "He feeds oxygen to the stripped atoms. Apparently some of them turned into hydrogen!" he added. "Don't you see, that's where the water came from!"

Both Lori and Barry stared at their friend, convinced that he was rambling incoherently about something related to his work at the hatcheries.

"What water, Ty?" Lori asked uncritically.

"The water I noticed when we stole the box the first time," Tyler said. He snapped his fingers. "That's what this connector is for," he added. He turned to Lori. "Do you have an oxygen bottle?"

"Sure. It's behind Barry."

"Get it, Barry."

When he was handed the bottle, Tyler examined it closely, then looked at Lori. "Do you have a mask and stuff--"

"Yes, and the tube --." Tyler looked back and saw Barry rummaging behind the seat. Waiting, he studied the box as though determining dimensions or sizing something. He turned just as Barry came up with a mask and its tubing and connector. "Great. We need to cut --"

"Here," Barry said, offering a small pocketknife.

Tyler worked rapidly, cutting the hose and fitting it over the small connector in the small panel of the box. He attached the other end to the oxygen bottle. "Give me your belt, Barry." he requested, still studying the bottle.

Without hesitation, Barry stripped his belt and passed it to the front, a wry smirk on his face. Tyler placed the bottle along the side of the box and drew it tight with the belt. He finally sat back, a pleased look about him.

Looking at the box and the attached bottle, Barry shook his head. "I don't get it, man," he admitted.

Lori nodded in agreement.

Tyler instructed Barry to cut the box's cable near the connector and strip all the wires.

"Now, just twist all the wires together. They are the control lines, and maybe this will turn them all on. It's a long shot, but it's all we have."

Lori suddenly applied full throttle and pulled the plane in a tight climb. Tyler and Barry were slammed back. "What are you --?"

"I'm trying to lose him in those clouds," Lori yelled, "and if we can get back near Clarksburg --"

"Watch out!" Barry screamed.

The Mooney had swung wide and was turning toward them, and was so close that Tyler saw the gun protrude from a small panel in Rossiter's window. The gun spewed flame.

Bullets snapped through the thin aluminum and cracks appeared in the Plexiglas windows. Lori screamed and ducked forward. Barry grunted and grabbed his shoulder. "I'm hit," he yelled.

Lori saw blood running down Tyler's cheek. "Ty! You're hurt, too," she yelled, sobbing.

"I'm fine!" Tyler assured her, "just a sliver." He asked Barry how serious it was.

"Just a scratch," Barry whispered as he grimaced.

The radio crackled with Rossiter's voice. "I told you, no tricks. Next time I'll kill you all. Start your descent. I'll be right behind you. Keep your airspeed at ninety, slow to seventy before flare and touchdown."

"I know how to land my plane," Lori snapped. "Then what?"

"Go to the end of the runway and shut off your engine. If you try to take off, I will catch you and shoot you out of the sky. Now, when you land, Miss Dennison, you get out and walk toward my plane. Otherwise, I will riddle your plane with bullets. Do you understand?" His voice was alien, strange and remote.

"I think he'll do it, too," Tyler said, dabbing his cheek. "He sounds crazy enough."

Guiding the plane toward the small asphalt strip, Lori glanced at Tyler. "I'm scared," she said.

"Don't worry." Tyler's voice was filled with confidence. Lori smiled and relaxed, settling slightly in her seat.

As the plane skimmed then settled on the runway, Tyler looked at both people. "Lori, do as he says. Barry, scrunch down in the seat. Maybe he's forgotten about you. Besides, if he starts shooting, being on the floor might save your life." He grasped Lori's hand. "Stay to the side of him if you can, Lori. Barry, give me that little package back there."

Barry handed a bundle of cloth up front. Tyler unwrapped the cloth, exposing the piece broken from the meteorite. He carefully stuffed it in his back pocket.

"You want my gun?" Barry asked.

"No, keep it with you. I'll need both hands."

Lori taxied her plane to the end as instructed, and turned off the engine. In a few seconds they heard the approaching motor of the Mooney. When it shut down, Lori looked at Tyler and opened her door. She stepped down, and started walking back toward Rossiter's aircraft.

As Lori approached, remembering what Tyler had told her, she walked wide, toward the right wingtip. Reaching it, she stopped.

Rossiter opened his door and stepped out on the wing. He was armed with an automatic pistol. He motioned for Lori to step around behind the wing. As she complied, he stepped down.

Through a cracked door, Tyler watched the two people and cursed softly. Rossiter was behind the wing! He could never get close enough to disarm him!

"Bridges! You and your friend get out of the plane!" he shouted.

Tyler quickly slid to the ground and held the box at arm's length above his head, the oxygen bottle out of Rossiter's line of vision. Barry climbed out the other side.

"You," he pointed the gun toward Barry, "put your hands on your head. Now, you two get together in front of her plane . . . now!"

He held the gun close to Lori's head. "Now, walk toward me and put the box on the wing."

Tyler hesitated and Rossiter, visibly angry, grabbed Lori's arm and put the gun to her temple. "Do as I say, or I'll splatter her brains all over this runway!" he shouted through clenched teeth. "No more Mexican standoffs this time, Bridges!" he cried. Quickly he grabbed Lori's neck and steered her around the end of the wing and took a step toward Tyler. "We'll get closer so you can see her die better." He laughed, an insane gurgle that sounded animal-like. His eyes, dark and glistening, showed the frustration, the utter desperation of the man, that he was truly ready to kill whether or not he obtained his device.

"You're close to having your box, Rossiter, so don't do anything foolish," Tyler interjected.

Tyler approached Rossiter, and extended the device in front of him. Rossiter's eyes ranged from Lori to Tyler to Barry. "Place it on the wing," he snapped, pulling Lori to the side.

As he started to set the box down, Rossiter frowned. "What's that thing --?"

At that instant, Tyler flipped the knob to its fullest position.

The device hissed as the oxygen tank dumped its charge. The box began spinning crazily then shot skyward with the speed of a rifle bullet.

"No!" shouted Rossiter. His eyes followed the wild gyrations, now almost out of site. Seeing this, Barry pulled his revolver at the same instant that Rossiter returned his eyes to earth. He swung his pistol at Southerland, flames bursting from the weapon. Tyler yanked the rock from his pocket and threw it to the asphalt at Rossiter's feet. The rock burst into tiny pieces, and a dust cloud soared upward and disappeared into the older man's abdomen.

Suddenly he raised on his tiptoes, grunted as he sucked in his chest, pulled his shoulders forward as though struck in the solar plexus, and fell dead on the asphalt.

All three suddenly looked skyward, prompted by a small explosion and vibration. "Sonic," Tyler said aloud. They saw a pinpoint of light then a brilliant flash.

Lori, sobbing, hugged Tyler, then broke away and ran to Barry. He was grasping his shoulder from the first bullet, but didn't appear injured otherwise. "I'm fine, kids," he told them as they approached. "Help me in the plane and get me to an emergency room."

Lori wasted no time dragging the Cessna around to point it generally toward the far end of the runway. Tyler grabbed Rossiter's automatic pistol then helped Barry into the plane. Within minutes, she had coaxed the engine to life, and after a slight warm up and checkout, steered the plane around the Mooney, picked up speed, lifted off and angled upward into the sky.

Barry sat quietly, pressing a cloth against his shoulder. Lori glanced at Tyler, who was looking back across their path, deep in with thoughts of what she knew not.

After landing in Elkins, Tyler rushed Barry to the hospital, where he was treated for a gunshot wound that, the attendants were told, occurred accidentally at a shooting range.

Robin Southerland was notified, and after showing up with a barrage of questions about his activities lately, she drove Barry home.

"You drive back," Tyler told Lori, then slumped into the front seat.

At the wheel, Lori glanced toward Tyler and saw the empty stare, the head scratching, the eyebrow pulling. "What is it?"

Seeing no response, Lori knew her passenger had been drawn deep into his obsessive thought. At the moment, the world did not exist for him; the reality of the moment was postponed. Everything was on hold pending some breakthrough from the maze of thoughts and calculations swirling in Tyler's head.

"Ty? We're home," Lori told him while shaking him lightly. Then, with her lips pursed and eyebrows raised, she added: "We're at the church and the minister just pronounced us man and wife!"

Getting no response, she climbed out then opened his door quickly.

The sudden movement shocked Tyler from his thoughtful trance. "Oh, we're home. Why didn't you say something?"

Lori rolled her eyes and grabbed his arm and led him inside. "You're obsessing again, Ty. Want to tell me what's bugging you?" she asked.

Tyler stared a moment. "Gerald," he said thoughtfully. "Gerald Franks."

Chapter 21

On Sunday morning, Lori noticed that Tyler continued to be ensconced in his obsession about Gerald Franks. She thought about asking what it was all about, but decided that Tyler was taking Gerald's death hard, and would open up to her when the time was right. So she occupied herself with a book while Tyler sat moodily, feet across the chair arm, pulling his eyebrow and tapping his head rhythmically. Realizing that she was unable to break through his web of mystery and comtemplation, Lori finally conceded defeat and decided to go to the airport for some final preparations for her upcoming flights.

She finally got his attention. "Ty, I'm going home. Busy day tomorrow," she told him. She kissed him on the forehead, promised to call him after her flights on Monday, and left.

Tyler watched until her car was out of site, then, as though released from some mental bondage, he went inside, threw some some items in a backpack, left the house and headed south. As he started, the late afternoon sun had slipped far below the mountaintops, casting long shadows across the flatlands. In his preoccupied state, Tyler navigated the highway by instinct, his eyes seeing only the twisting, winding road approaching him. His thoughts were far away, and in a different time.

By the time he reached Gerald's house, darkness had fallen in the deep valley of Green Bank. He noticed that for all outward appearances, the house was abandoned. The yard had not been mowed, and his old roommate's car was parked around the side, showing no signs of being moved since the memorial service, and no inside lights were visible. Tyler stood at the front stoop and looked around. It was quiet. There was a large picture window to his left, and a small window on the other side. Tyler knocked on the door and immediately saw a slight movement of a curtain beside the door.

He waited a moment, then knocked again. He tried the knob. The door was locked.

"It's Tyler. Let me in," he said softly.

He heard the click and the door opened slightly. Bridges stepped in through the crack.

Gerald Franks quickly pushed the door closed and snapped the lock. He turned on a dim overhead light, and motioned Tyler into the room.

Tyler shot Gerald a hard, serious look, and tossed his backpack on a chair. "I ought to punch you in the nose, man. Now, what the hell is going on? You almost got us all killed.

Franks looked both guilty and scared. He gestured for Tyler to sit, and took a chair himself. "How did you know?" he finally asked.

"I didn't," said Tyler, "but things just didn't add up in my mind. The funeral, for one. Some other mysterious things going on. All this code stuff seemed too dramatic to me."

"Yeh," Gerald said, shaking his head, "the memorial service was hard to pull off. Had some help from a couple of friends. But, the code worked, didn't it?" He smiled quickly, then abandoned it when he saw the look on his old roommate's face.

"Why, Gerald?" Tyler asked.

"Because they tried to kill me, Ty. Two attempts. They took a shot at me one night, and later they tried to knife me. The shot missed, and whoever struck at me with a knife disappeared in the darkness before I could see anything." He sighed wearily. "I had to hide out for a while."

"Who are 'they'?" Tyler asked.

"Rossiter or Leif, or their hired killer, I suppose. So, I faked my death." He grunted. "Figured it would buy me some time to figure out what to do. Turns out, Rossiter is dead, so I guess I'm safe now."

"Who told you Rossiter was dead?"

"Sidney Tarrant. He said they found his body at some airport. You have anything to do with that, Ty?"

"I figure you already know the answer to that, Gerald. Hell, you helped me get away from the plant a couple of times, didn't you?"

He shook his head and looked down. "Yes. After I had staged my death, I got to thinking that I may have put you and your friends in harms way, so I contacted Barry Southerland and he kept me apprised of your movements. I knew when you were going to try to steal the machine, so I hid in the woods behind the plant, and, well, you know the rest. I shot out a tire the first time, and managed to keep Rossiter off your backs the last time."

"Who was Rossiter, and how did you get mixed up in this, Gerald?"

Franks sat back in his chair. "Kyle Rossiter was my uncle by marriage. One of Mom's sisters. Anyway, I was working for the company when I happened to discover a meteorite that Rossiter had obtained. I accidentally stumbled onto the unstable nature of it, and began to develop what I called

'The Zero Mass Machine'. Uncle Kyle was thrilled, and he moved me downstairs where he and I worked on the unit privately and secretly. One day I overheard him talking on the telephone. He was plotting to market the device to terrorists. I confronted him about it and we had a violent argument, and I threatened to call the authorities.

"He somehow had found out that I was once involved in a scheme to embezzle money from JBL in California. He threatened to turn me in if I didn't go along with him. He had the power and wherewith all to do it, too. I didn't want to go to prison." Gerald wrung his hands, and walked around the room. "For the first time in my life, Ty, I didn't know what to do, where to turn. I agreed not to say anything, but refused to continue working on the unit. That's when he sent me here to Green Bank. He arranged for me to take a peon job here so he could keep a watch over me. He paid me a little, so with my salary here, I was living a pretty good life. I didn't hear from him, the money kept coming in, so I forgot about the device. You know, 'out of site, out of mind'. Then, when I retrieved the meteorite from Dennison, I thought that might put me in a better light, that maybe I could still talk him out of it, so I tried." Gerald shook his head thoughtfully. "Didn't work. In fact, I think that's when he decided to eliminate me, figuring I would go to the authorities sooner or later. I don't think he wanted to kill me, but he was getting real desperate. The buyers were getting impatient."

Tyler sat quietly, his eyes following the man as he walked around the room.

"I had made friends with Sidney Tarrant," he went on, "so I told him all about it and had him help me with the fake memorial service. I guess Rossiter sent Craig Lynch to my memorial service. Apparently he was convinced of my death. I figured he would report back to Uncle Kyle, and that would be the end of it.

He snorted. "Apparently the funeral thing didn't work, or he found out somehow, but someone tried to kill me." Gerald forced a quick laugh then looked at Tyler for confirmation. "But now that Rossiter is dead, everything's all right. Isn't it?"

"I don't know, Gerald, It would seem so." Tyler retrieved his backpack and extracted the drawings for the device. He handed them to Gerald. "Here are your drawings and notes. What are your plans now, Gerald? Going to try to rebuild your machine? I'm sure another meteorite will come along sooner or later."

Franks walked to the desk and carefully removed a small rock the size of a golf ball. He placed it on the coffee table with caution. Both men looked at it knowingly. Finally Tyler looked up and spoke. "So? You've got the plans -- and the fuel. What do you do now?"

"I'm going to destroy everything, the plans and the rock. I don't think we're ready for anything like this right now. Besides, there will always be a Rossiter, and there will always be terrorists and criminals wanting to rule the world or get rich at any cost."

Tyler started for the door. "Hell of a loss," he said, "but I think it's the right thing to do, Jer. I'm still pissed at you for endangering all of us, buddy, but I guess 'all's well that ends well,' applies here. At least I got out of my financial hole," he said, looking back, "and hooked up with an old college buddy."

As Tyler opened the door he stopped suddenly, and began backing up, staring downward.

"Good evening, gentlemen," the voice said, stepping into the room. Sidney Tarrant held the gun steady, dropped a key into his pocket, and motioned the two men to sit down on the couch. Tyler watched as a big bearded man moved catlike into the room. He glanced around quickly, saw the closed curtains and the single overhead light and spoke: "Now, Gerald, I want the plans and drawings --"

His eyes came to rest on the coffee table as he spotted the stack of papers Tyler had brought. A slight malicious smile crossed his lips. "Sorry, Gerald," he whispered, "but some people I know need these plans badly -- and right away."

"It was you trying to kill me? Why, Sidney?" Gerald asked.

Tarrant began gathering the papers and stuffing them inside his coat. "Because you're the only one who knew about the terrorist deal. You see, I found out about your little embezzlement deal and told Rossiter. He promised me a piece of the action, since I supplied him with the information he needed to keep you quiet. So you see? I can't have you and your friend here running around the country telling everybody about this, can I? Now," he growled, "both of you, on the floor, hands behind you."

As the two men slowly laid down, Tarrant moved toward the curtains and began digging in his pocket. He pulled out a roll of duct tape.

Gerald glanced at Tyler and began laughing, giggling like a teenage girl. "At least he won't get the fuel," he whispered.

Tarrant barely heard the remark. He slanted his head. "What? What fuel?" He ran to Gerald and placed the gun at his head. "I said, what fuel?"

"Tell him!" Tyler screamed. "If you don't, I will!"

Tarrant immediately shifted his gun. "What fuel?"

"OK. OK!" Gerald yelled. "It's -- on the coffee table."

Tarrant glanced around. "What? Where?"

Both men remained quiet. Then Gerald giggled.

Tarrant cocked the revolver. "You have three seconds!"

"Alright! It's the small rock, there. It makes the fuel for the machine."

"If you're lying --!" the lawyer said as he grabbed the rock.

Gerald's eyes opened wide. "Wait, you don't understand! It's radioactive!"

In the span of the next instant, two events took place: Tarrant dropped the rock. When it struck the coffee table it released millions of zero-mass atoms which broke the vacuum of the overhead light bulb, causing it to explode, plunging the room into darkness.

In the pitch black darkness, Tyler heard Gerald move toward the big man and heard them both fall. Then he heard a loud thump as both men hit the floor. As he scrambled to his feet to assist Gerald, a light flashed and a muffled explosion hit his ears.

Tyler scrambled in the now-quiet darkness until he found a lamp. He snapped the switch.

Gerald was slowly climbing from beneath the big mass on the floor. He stood up, panting, looking down., the sweat shining on his forehead.

"You OK?" Tyler asked.

"I'm fine," Gerald answered, still staring down and breathing hard. Then he gestured at Tyler. "Ty, get out of here. I think Tarrant is dead. I'll tell the cops he came in here and tried to rob me."

"I don't know --," Tyler stammered.

"Just go on. I'll be fine." He grabbed Tyler's backpack and shoved it against his chest. "I'll be fine. Don't worry. I'll give you a call. Now, go!"

Tyler allowed himself to be shoved out the door. "Radioactive? Jer, you're a genius."

"You don't have to tell me. I know it," Gerald said, smiling. "Now go!"

On the way home, Tyler kept thinking about Lori Dennison. He missed her immensely. Even more so lately. She kept the feelings of loneliness and abandonment from overtaking him.

It was late when he finally pulled into his driveway. Inside, he tossed his backpack in the corner and went to the phone. Lori answered after the second ring.

"Lori? It's me. Just wanted you to know I'm home. Come over?

"Be right there," came the voice. Tyler smiled in contentment when he hung up. She would be there in twenty minutes, and everything would be all right then.

Lori sat wide-eyed as Tyler told her what had happened at Green Bank and that Gerald was still alive. When he finished, she hugged him hard. "Oh, Ty. I'm so happy that your friend isn't dead. It's wonderful!" she beamed, then she pulled away, and looked up in thought. "I know just the girl who will be perfect for him!"

Tyler smiled and took a deep breath. "We'll talk about that later."

The next morning, the story of Rossiter's death appeared in the local papers. Tyler called to Lori, who was busy in the kitchen, making noises with the breakfast dishes.

"Hey. Listen to this," he said, rattling the paper. 'Kyle Rossiter, founder of Rossiter Dynamics in Flatwoods, was found dead on a small airfield near Philippi on Sunday. Officials say he evidently suffered a seizure or heart attack and made an emergency landing. Rossiter apparently died after climbing out of his airplane. There was evidence of electrocution, possibly due to a lightning strike, although there were no storms reported in the area. No further details are available.'

Lori came in looking serious. "It's awful. Maybe he was a bad man, but to die like that --" She shook her head. "By the way, how's Barry?"

"Just talked to him. He's fine. Not near so much worried about his shoulder as he is of Robin. I think he's afraid she's going to turn him across her knee and spank him!"

Lori laughed heartily. "Love to see that," she quipped.

"Charters today?" Tyler asked.

"Uh huh," she answered. "Gotta' fly three people to a conference in Charleston. Be back this evening."

After Lori's flights, Tyler met her at the airport and they had dinner before returning to Tyler's.

When they came in, the answering machine had a message from Craig Lynch. Lori punched the button on the device then left the room.

"Mister Bridges, this is Craig Lynch. I hope you remember me. As a new stockholder, I'm sure you are somewhat concerned as to what will happen to Rossiter Dynamics now that Mister Rossiter is no longer with us. I'm here to tell you that we will continue to operate as always, and that a new product line of automobile automation, as well as our military contracts, will secure our future for many years to come. Mister Gerald Franks, whom I think you know, will return to our engineering staff soon, and I'm sure he will have a positive impact on our new product lines. If you have any questions about your stock, please feel free to call me. Goodbye."

After Lori had helped Tyler get comfortable on the couch, she showered and changed clothes. She swirled into the living room and listened to the Lynch message on the phone.

"Did you ever find out who was following us besides Barry?"

"Yes. I think Gerald hired Tarrant, not knowing at the time that Tarrant was after the meteorite and the plans, too. I think he knew I would try to get my rock back, and just wanted to help us."

"That was nice of him, don't you think?" Lori said thoughtfully, coming over to the couch.

"Well, it kept me from punching him in the nose."

Lori frowned. "What's that mean?"

"Oh, nothing. Nothing at all." Then he took a deep breath. "By the way, did I ever mention that I wanted to marry you?"

Lori shook her head thoughtfully. "I mean, that man Rossiter's dead, Barry got wounded, now you almost get hurt by that lawyer – what did you say?"

"I guess I asked if you would marry me."

"Well," she said, fluffing her hair and straightening her skirt, "I, uh, suppose – yes," she said. Then her eyes shined, and she stared unbelieving at Tyler. "Oh, yes!" she exclaimed, "oh, very much yes!"

At that moment, Barry called. When Lori finished her narrative on the events of the past two days, Barry told her he would be right over.

"Oh, please don't," she pleaded, looking at a confused Tyler. "Tyler and I will be busy for a day or two . . . no, no, everything's all right. I'll let you know about the wedding. Bye." She hung up, giggling. "That'll drive him crazy!"

"You know," she said thoughtfully, "that zero mass thingy had possibilities. Imagine us making love, suspended above the city on a moonless night, floating there for hours and hours --."

"Sorry. Best I can do is up there in the loft," Tyler said, then he kissed her hard, pulling her body close.

Outside, a cool summer wind rustled the trees, their leaves gently scraping the large window at Tyler's loft.

10000853R0

Made in the USA
Lexington, KY
16 June 2011